Hey, peoples!

Nanika atta! (That basically means, "What's up, guys!" in Japanese.) Carly here! I'm inviting you to flip through the latest installment in the World iHistory of *iCarly*. That's right, people of Earth, *iCarly* has infiltrated the entire planet—next stop, Jupiter!

Spanning the globe makes for awesome news, and I hope lots of viewers in all different kinds of places are tuning in to *iCarly*. (Imagine what we'd sound like if *iCarly* were translated into other languages. . . . Can you say "*Mademoiselle Carly?*") Going international was a bit of a challenge. We had to make sure that my brother, Spencer, didn't insult everyone with his language skills (or lack thereof), and that my best friend, Sam, didn't spend the whole time looking for the overseas equivalent of low-fat Fat Cakes (yum!). So grab your passport, and start turning those pages to see how our first international *iCarly* adventure went. And don't forget to check out the amazing pictures, too! I'd write more, but traveling makes me sleepy, especially through different time zones. Did you know Japan is like almost a full day ahead of us here in Seattle? Fluffy pillow, here I come! ☺

Remember to keep watching *iCarly*—bye for now!

Carly

iGo to Japan!

Adapted by Aaron Rosenberg

Based on "iGo to Japan!" Parts 1–3

Teleplay by Dan Scheider
Story by Andrew Hill Newnan

iCarly TV Series
Created by Dan Schneider

SCHOLASTIC INC.

New York Toronto London Auckland
Sydney   Mexico City New Delhi Hong Kong

ISBN: 978-0-545-16218-0

Published by Scholastic Inc.
SCHOLASTIC and associated logos are trademarks and/or registered trademarks of Scholastic Inc.

12 11 10 9 8 7 6 5 4 3 2 1   10 11 12 13 14 15/ 0

Printed in the U.S.A
First printing, January 2010

iGo to Japan!

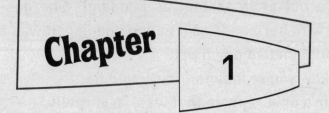

Chapter 1

"Legs."

"Pudding."

"Legs!"

"Pudding!"

"LEGS!"

"PUU-DDDINNGGGG!"

Carly shook her head, dark hair flying about her. She couldn't resist laughing. She and Sam were swinging back and forth on swings they'd just installed in their studio. They were in the middle of one of their most popular *iCarly* segments, "Random Debate." This one was about which was better, legs or pudding. Leave it to Sam to side with the food!

"Come on," Carly told her best friend, "legs are really important."

"I'm not saying legs aren't important," Sam replied, swinging past her. "What I'm saying is they're not as important as pudding!" She gestured with her hands as if eating pudding. It was a motion Sam had down pat.

"Okay, you're insane," Carly told her.

Sam's only reply to that was, "Not really."

"Without legs," Carly pointed out, "pants would be like, 'duh, now what do we do?'"

"Objection!" Sam shouted. "Pants can't talk." She looked smug. Off to the side, their other best friend, Freddie, laughed. He was busy video-taping the entire debate, of course. That's how *iCarly* worked, after all—Carly and Sam were the ones on-screen and Freddie took care of the filming, the uploading, and all the technical stuff.

"Why are we swinging?" Carly demanded.

"I don't know!" Sam admitted.

Carly took that as an opportunity to hop off her swing. "Okay!" she announced to the camera. "This Random Debate is over!"

Sam hopped off and leaped in front of her, her long, dark blond hair somehow neatly in place. "I won!" she announced.

"No," Carly corrected her. "We're going to let the *iCarly* viewers decide who won." That was half the fun of doing a Web show — their viewers could actually vote right away.

"Fine," Sam agreed. "Everyone at iCarly-dot-com, look at the homepage and vote on what you think is more important —"

"Legs," Carly cut in.

"— or pudding!" Sam finished.

Carly leaned forward and grabbed the camera lens. "If you don't vote," she told their viewers, trying to look stern, "you don't care."

Just then a bell began ringing. The lights dimmed and disco strobe lights flashed on.

"Random Dancing!" a deep voice declared.

This was another regular feature on the show. If the voice said dancing, well, it was time to dance! Carly and Sam began rocking to the beat. Even Freddie was bopping along, which of course meant the camera was moving all over the place. But that was part of the fun.

Carly and Sam did the Robot and several other goofball dance moves before the music faded and the lights came back up. "Okay, later!" Carly told the camera.

"Pudding!" Sam declared, pointing at the viewers menacingly.

"Legs, vote now!" Carly encouraged her supporters.

"iCarly-dot-com," Sam reminded.

"Bye!" Carly started waving, and Sam joined in. They both waved and shouted good-byes as Freddie backed up to his Pearbook laptop, which ran the Webcast.

"And . . . we're clear," he declared, hitting the STOP button on the laptop and lowering the camera.

"Yeah!" Carly and Sam high-fived.

"Good show," Freddie agreed.

"Okay, let's go downstairs and snack it up!" Sam declared. It always amazed Carly that her friend could make it through their half-hour show without eating something. Many times, she didn't — Carly had lost track of the number of times Sam had snuck food during their Webcasts. Fortunately, their viewers knew all about Sam's immense appetite, so they totally understood.

Sam headed downstairs, and Carly started to follow her, but stopped as she realized Freddie was still fiddling with the laptop. "You coming?" she asked him.

"You guys go ahead," he told her. "I've got some . . . tech stuff to wrap up." They had been friends for years, so Carly knew Freddie wasn't telling the truth. She also had a pretty good idea why.

"You want to play on the swing?" she asked him with a smile.

"Will you push me?" he replied.

She didn't even have to think about that one. "Yes!"

They raced for the swings.

"Any votes come in yet?" Sam asked a few minutes later, as Freddie and Carly joined her down in the kitchen. The fact that their studio was set up in the upper floor of Carly and her brother, Spencer's, loft certainly made their lives easier!

"Give me a second!" Freddie complained. He climbed onto one of the bar stools and slid the wireless keyboard over so he could pull up the *iCarly* site. Carly hopped onto the stool next to him. Sam, of course, was already at the refrigerator.

"You know legs are going to beat pudding," Carly warned as she and Freddie waited for their site to update.

"Don't bet on it," Sam replied. Her attention was quickly drawn to the contents of the fridge, however. "Who wants a snack?" she called over her shoulder.

"I'm good," Carly told her.

"Toss me an apple?" Freddie asked, still watching the screen.

"Red or green?" was Sam's follow-up question as she made her way back from the fridge, soda and chocolate pudding in hand. The basket of fruit was on the table and conveniently along her path.

"Red," Freddie told her. "Because green apples always seem —" Whatever else he'd been about to say was cut off as Sam hurled a red apple straight at his head. The apple nailed Freddie solidly in the left temple, knocking him off the stool and to the floor!

"Sorry," Sam claimed as she joined them at

the counter. "I put a little too much heat on that." She didn't seem overly apologetic, but then Sam always enjoyed hitting or hurting Freddie. It was one of her favorite pastimes.

"Ah!" Freddie hauled himself back up to his seat, hand pressed to his forehead. "Do you see what you did?"

"You should have asked for a muffin," Carly said. Really, why didn't Freddie ever learn? "Bring up the votes!" she urged him, both because she was curious and to distract him from his latest injury.

"Okay." Freddie brought up the "Random Debate" voting window. "Looks like we've got about twelve thousand votes," he reported, "and legs are ahead of pudding by about twenty percent." It always amazed Carly just how many people watched their show!

But right now she was just happy she was winning. "Hah!" she declared.

"Idiots!" was Sam's response. She took another bite of her pudding, apparently unfazed by its defeat.

"Oh hey, we got a v-mail," Freddie announced.

Carly was intrigued. "Who from?"

"I don't know — someone in England."

"Cool!"

"Play it," Sam ordered. Freddie obligingly clicked on it, and the message took over the screen. They saw a man sitting at a desk — he was wearing a blue button-down shirt and had silvery gray hair. A name plaque in front of him read "Theodore Wilkins," and several award statues stood on his desk and on a table behind him. They were shaped like a lower-case "i" with the word "Web" carved into them.

"Greetings, *iCarly*," the man announced with one of those cheery British accents Carly remembered from *Mary Poppins*. "My name is Theodore Wilkins. I'm the vice-chairman of the iWeb awards, an international competition which seeks out the best Web shows on the Internet. And I am very pleased to announce that our committee has nominated *iCarly* in the category of Best Comedy."

"Whoa!" Freddie burst out.

"We're nominated for Best Comedy Web show!" Sam added.

"I know," Carly agreed. "I speak British!"

"The iWeb awards would like to fly the *iCarly* team overseas," Mr. Wilkins continued, "so that your show can compete at this year's live competition." He smiled. "All expenses paid, of course."

"This is insane!" Freddie declared.

"They're going to fly us overseas!" Carly enthused.

"If you accept your nomination," Mr. Wilkins was saying, "please click on the ACCEPT button in the lower left corner of this v-mail." As if by magic, a big blue button appeared there, the word "Accept" stamped across it.

"Come on, click on it," Carly urged. Sam joined in.

"I'm clicking!" Freddie assured them, mousing over to the button and clicking it.

Mr. Wilkins nodded as the ACCEPT button disappeared. "Your invitation, passes, and travel itinerary will be sent off to you tomorrow," he informed them. "Congratulations, *iCarly* — see you at the iWeb awards."

"All right!" Carly, Sam, and Freddie all high-fived one another and whooped and cheered.

"Okay, this is the biggest thing that's ever happened to us," Carly enthused.

"By far!" Freddie agreed.

"Ever!" was Sam's contribution.

The v-mail window closed, leaving the "Random Debates" window in front again. "Oh, check it out." Freddie couldn't resist needling Sam. "Way more people are voting for legs than pudding."

"Told ya!" Carly taunted.

Sam still didn't seem too concerned. "All I know is," she commented, scooping some pudding onto her spoon and raising it in front of her, "you can't do this with legs." And she whipped the spoon forward, splattering pudding all over Freddie's face.

Freddie just sat there, frozen.

"Uh," Carly said, "you've got a little pudding . . ."

"I see it," he assured her. It would have been hard for him not to — it was completely covering his left eye!

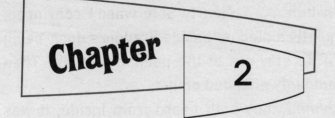
"Hey," Sam asked as they rounded the corner to Carly's loft after school, "do you think Freddie's home from school yet?" Freddie and his mom, Mrs. Benson, lived right across the hall from Carly and Spencer.

"Yeah, he got a ride," Carly answered absently. "Why?" She was busy wondering why they hadn't received anything from Mr. Wilkins yet. It had been a week! She'd asked Lewbert at the front desk but he'd only shrieked at her. He was like that.

Sam smirked. "Betcha he's lookin' through his peephole, waitin' for you to get home."

"*Nooo*, he grew outta that." In the past, Freddie had admitted that he had a massive crush on Carly. She'd told him any number of times that she only liked him as a friend, but that never stopped him from hoping — or from following her around like a little lost puppy.

"Uh-huh. . . ." Clearly Sam wasn't convinced. She quietly sidled up beside Freddie's door, being careful to stay out of the peephole's view. Then she suddenly pounded on it.

"*Ahhhh!*" they both heard from inside. It was unmistakably Freddie.

Sam started laughing, but Carly was concerned. That had sounded like it hurt!

The door opened a second later, and Freddie stumbled out, one hand pressed to his forehead.

"'Sup?" Sam asked him, still laughing.

Freddie glared at her for a second, then turned to Carly. "I was not looking out my peephole, waiting for you to come home," he assured her.

"I know you weren't," Carly told him. She turned toward her front door. But she couldn't resist giving him trouble. "Peeper."

"What?" Freddie demanded. Carly just shrugged and unlocked her door. Sam and Freddie followed her in.

"Okay," Carly wondered out loud as they all stepped inside, "why is it dark in here?"

"Because!" a voice announced somewhere farther in the apartment. A bright light suddenly flared, blinding the three of them for a second. When they could see again, they discovered Carly's brother, Spencer, standing in the middle of the room with a strange contraption strapped to his head. It looked like a hard hat with wires and fuses running all around it, and something like a motorcycle headlight mounted on the front. That's where the light was from. "I made this!" Spencer declared, pointing up at the strange device. He looked really pleased with himself.

Carly shook her head. "Why?" she asked.

Spencer was a sculptor by trade, but an inventor by choice. He came up with strange devices all the time. She just usually couldn't see what good they'd do anyone.

"It's for jogging at night," Spencer explained. "This baby puts out over nineteen thousand lumens!" He grinned at her. "It could light up a football field!"

"For how long?" Freddie asked, walking over to examine it. As their resident techie, Freddie was the one most often interested in Spencer's crazy inventions.

"'Til its battery runs out," Spencer answered. He turned to the side and now they could see the massive battery strapped to his back. It said "Heavy Duty" in bold letters and had wires running up to the helmet. "I got it out of a Prius!"

Just then there was a knock on their door. Carly was the closest, so she answered it.

"Oh, hi, Mrs. Benson," Carly said as she opened it. Freddie's mom smiled at her.

"Mom, what are you still doing here?" Freddie asked her. "I thought you left for your pottery class?" Carly detected a note of worry in his voice. Mrs. Benson was a nice lady, but she was super-protective — it was a struggle each day for Freddie to get her to let him out of their loft! Her pottery classes and seminars were some of the only times Freddie had to himself. He cherished each and every second.

Mrs. Benson shrugged. "I tried to," she admitted, "but my Prius wouldn't start." On the other side of the room, Spencer suddenly looked a little

14

embarrassed as Freddie glared at him. So that's where he'd gotten the battery!

"Anyway," Mrs. Benson continued, "I forgot — this package addressed to *iCarly* came in the mail yesterday—"

Carly stared at her, and at the large, white SendEx box she was holding up. "Yesterday!" she yelped. And she'd been worrying that it had gotten lost somehow!

"I'm sorry!" Mrs. Benson stammered. "I meant to tell Freddie, but—"

Sam ripped the box from her hand and raced toward the kitchen counter. Carly and Freddie took off after her.

"Is that from the iWeb Awards?" Spencer asked as Sam set the package on the counter and the three of them clustered around it.

"Uh-huh, yep!" Carly told him over her shoulder. She'd told her brother all about it, of course — he was her legal guardian, after all. But they were also great friends, and he was *iCarly*'s biggest supporter. No way was she not going to tell him about something that exciting!

15

"C'mon," Freddie demanded behind her as she opened it and pulled out a bunch of folders and papers, "what country are we goin' to?!"

Carly scanned the papers . . . and her face fell. "Uhhhhh . . ." She looked up at her friends. "Canada."

Sam and Freddie looked at her, and at each other.

"Canada?" Sam repeated. They lived in Seattle! Canada was right over the border! They could go there anytime!

Carly let them suffer for a few seconds more before she broke into a big smile. "Just kiddin' — TOKYO! We're goin' to JAPAN!"

Sam started screaming, and Freddie and Carly joined in. They jumped around and high-fived and hugged each other.

"Uh, Freddie, you can let go now," Carly reminded him after his hug lasted a little too long.

"Oh, right." He let her go and stepped back a bit.

Spencer was looking at the information from the package. "Sweet!" he said. "Y'know, I took a year of Japanese in college. A little brush up and I'll be speakin' Japanese like a" — he paused, searching for the right word — "Japanesiologist." Carly's brother never let his lack of knowledge stop him. Ever.

Mrs. Benson didn't look too happy, however. She snatched the papers from Spencer and glanced at them. "Freddie, I'm not sure I can allow this," she warned.

"Here we go," Sam sighed. She wasn't particularly fond of Freddie's mother.

Right now, Freddie wasn't happy with her either. "Mom!" he protested.

"It's just Japan," Carly tried to assure her. But for Mrs. Benson, worrying too much was a way of life.

"Right," she told Carly, "which is why I worry that . . . y'know, the Far East can be very. . ." She sighed in frustration. "Look, just because I can't think of anything right now doesn't mean Japan isn't fraught with danger." She was still clutching one of the folders, and her hands tightened around it — Carly was afraid she was going to wring its neck!

Sam had had enough. "*Ulch*, c'mon lady!" she shouted.

"It's okay," Spencer tried to reassure Mrs. Benson. "I'm goin' with 'em. So it's not like they won't have a responsible adult making sure everything goes smoothly."

Freddie nodded beside Spencer, and Carly and Sam tried to look confident as well. Mrs. Benson's frown lessened just a notch.

Unfortunately, Spencer's headlight hat chose that exact moment to burst into flames.

Everybody started screaming and gesturing. It took Spencer a second to realize why, and then he began screaming as well.

"Oh, put it out, put it out!" he pleaded. "Now! Go! Please!"

Sam grabbed a stack of hand towels from the kitchen table and tossed some to Freddie and Carly. The three of them descended upon Spencer, who was now crouching down so they could reach his flaming helmet, and they began beating the fire out. None of them were really surprised — for some reason most of Spencer's inventions burst into flames. Even the ones that had nothing to do with electricity or fire.

Finally the fire was out and Spencer sank down

onto one of the stools. Then he seemed to remember that Mrs. Benson was still standing there, looking horrified.

"So," he told her more quietly, "I'll make sure everything goes smoothly in Japan." His hat was still smoking.

Mrs. Benson shook her head. "Freddie, you're not going to Japan!" she declared. She grabbed his arm and headed for the door, dragging him with her. "You're coming home with me to take a bath."

"Wait!" Carly shouted, running after them. They couldn't go without Freddie! She spit out the first idea that popped into her head. "Why don't you come to Japan with us?"

"*Aaahhh*!" Sam screamed and stepped in front of Carly.

"What?" Carly demanded.

Sam glared at her. "I don't wanna take a trip across the world with that mess of a woman!"

"C'mon, Mrs. Benson," Spencer added, crossing the room to join the rest of them. "It'll be fun." He raised a hand to his ear as if taking a call, and gasped. "What's that? I think I hear Tokyo callin'

Toki-you!" He pointed at her and gave her his biggest smile.

"Come with us to Japan," Freddie urged his mom as Carly turned back to take another look at their information packets. "You love sushi!"

Mrs. Benson actually seemed to be weakening! "I suppose it would be nice to try a California roll from where it all started," she admitted.

Carly pulled the tickets out of the box. "Wait, hang on, we have a problem," she called out. She carried the tickets over to everyone else.

"What?" Spencer asked her.

"Three tickets," Carly answered, holding them up.

"Good!" Sam told her. Then she glanced back at Freddie and Mrs. Benson and shrugged. "I mean, oh no." Carly frowned, though. She knew there was no way Spencer would let her go without him, and she didn't even blame him. Three kids on their own in Japan? Not a good plan! But if Freddie couldn't go, the *iCarly* team wouldn't be complete, and that could be a disaster, too!

"Here, let me see them," Spencer told her. She handed them over and he scanned them. "Okay,

20

great!" he assured them after a second. "These are first-class tickets! I can just trade these for five coach seats and we're all set!"

Freddie turned to his mom, pleading all over his face.

"Oh, all right!" she agreed at last. "But if we're all going to Japan, there's a lot of preparation to be done. We'll need passports, fresh underwear, a voltage converter for your night-light . . ." She took Freddie's arm and headed for the door again as Carly and Sam laughed.

"I don't need a night-light anymore!" Freddie protested. But the look on his face said he wasn't telling the truth.

"Man, she's a piece a' work," Spencer laughed after they'd gone.

Then his headlight hat began burning again.

"Put it out, put it out!" Spencer begged as Sam and Carly grabbed their hand towels a second time. "Why does this keep happening to me?"

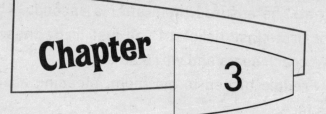

Chapter 3

"I know, Oompé," the man declared with a smirk. "If I had a haircut like yours, I would be embarrassed, too!" He laughed—well, sniggered, really—while the French-poodle hand puppet on his right hand studied him. Then they started barking at each other. They both wore berets.

Carly grimaced and glanced down at the information packet again. She, Sam, and Freddie were all sitting in their studio watching the show on one of their big screens—Carly on a chair with her legs propped up, Sam sprawled on a beanbag drinking a soda, and Freddie cross-legged, leaning against the beanbag with his laptop in his lap. "So this is Henri P'Twa and his poodle puppet Oompé," she told the others.

"That's the comedy show we're competing against?" Sam asked, making air quotes around the word "comedy."

"One of them," Freddie confirmed. They all watched in horror as the puppet proceeded to terrorize the man.

"Uh-oh," Sam offered. She didn't look overly concerned.

"Maybe Oompé should be neutered," Carly suggested. None of them were very impressed.

"Okay, so what's this other show we're competing against?" Sam asked a little while later, once they'd switched seats and Freddie had brought up more refreshments. It had taken him longer than expected to get them, and he'd muttered something about Spencer and a language-training program, complete with stand-up tutor, but had declined to say more.

"It's a Japanese Web show called *Kyoko and Yuki*," Carly told her after checking the packet.

"Japanese?" Sam asked.

"Great, then they'll have a home court advantage," Freddie complained.

"Just put their Web show on," Sam instructed him. "No one's paying you to look pretty."

"No one's paying me at all!" he retorted. But

they all knew he didn't mind. All three of them loved doing *iCarly*.

"Just click the thingie!" Carly urged to avoid another argument.

"Okay. *Kyoko and Yuki*." Freddie hit the button, and the new show filled their screen.

There was a pretty Japanese girl wearing a guitar and sobbing, begging the tall, wild-haired Japanese boy behind her to teach her how to play guitar. According to the packet, the girl was Kyoko and the boy was Yuki.

"You are the worst student I have ever taught!" Yuki roared at Kyoko. "Why do you play the guitar so poorly?"

"I don't know!" she wailed, raising her hands in anguish. Carly, Sam, and Freddie all started laughing — Kyoko's right hand was bigger than her head! She tried strumming the guitar, but her hand was as large as the instrument so it sounded awful. The kids laughed some more.

"Okay, they're kinda funny," Sam acknowledged.

"Definitely," Carly agreed.

"Well, yeah, but you guys are funnier," Freddie assured them both.

Carly smiled at him. "Thanks." Then she turned to Sam. "We just have to come up with something totally hilarious to do at the competition."

"Okay." Sam got up and paced a bit. "How about you and I play two kids at a birthday party trying to break open a piñata?" she suggested.

Carly sighed. "And let me guess—Freddie plays the piñata?"

"Yes!"

Freddie glared at her. "Why does every idea you have involve hitting me with a stick?" he demanded.

Sam shrugged.

"Come on," Carly told them both, "let's watch a little bit more so we know exactly what we're up against."

"I'm not worried," Sam stated as she returned to her seat. "Kyoko and Yuki aren't that funny!"

But when they resumed the video a bee appeared in the scene—and Kyoko began chasing after it, destroying the room as she began swatting everything in sight with her enormous hand. All three of the kids cracked up.

"Eh, I've seen funnier," Freddie claimed, though he wasn't very convincing.

"We'll beat those guys easily," Sam insisted, but she didn't sound all that sure either.

"All right, they're hilarious!" Carly voiced what they were all thinking. The three of them shared a look of concern. Clearly they were in for some real competition!

They watched a bit more—now Kyoko had Yuki over her knee and was spanking him with her huge hand. Carly couldn't stop laughing, and neither could Sam and Freddie.

"Okay," Carly finally managed. "Turn it off!" She took a quick gulp of water as Freddie froze the screen. "All right, let's face it," she announced after she'd swallowed, "Kyoko and Yuki are really funny." Freddie started to protest, and she shut him up with a gesture. "They're really funny!"

"So is *iCarly*." Sam assured her. "We're gonna win that iWeb award."

"Right." But Carly wasn't so sure. "And even if

we don't win," she continued, "I mean, it's still an honor just to be nominated, right?"

"Yeah," Freddie agreed. "And win or lose, we still get a free trip to Japan."

"Whoa, whoa!" Sam hopped up from her seat. "I don't wanna hear this 'or lose' talk, all right?"

Freddie frowned. "But I just meant that —"

Sam cut him off. "Saying 'or lose' is like giving up. Carly," she asked, "when Miss Briggs told us we couldn't pick the kids to be in the talent show, did you give up?"

"No," Carly admitted. That was how they'd wound up doing *iCarly* in the first place!

"And what about the time those cops were chasing me and yelling at me to stop running," Sam continued. "Did I give up?"

Carly laughed and shook her head. "No, you kept running."

"And Freddie," Sam demanded, "have you ever given up your hope that one day Carly might love you?"

Freddie blushed but straightened up. "No."

"Well, ya should," Sam told him. Leave it to Sam to slam Freddie in the middle of a motivational speech! "Anyway, we are gonna beat Kyoko and Yuki and win that iWeb award!"

Carly jumped up. "You're right! We just gotta come up with the funniest *iCarly* bit we've ever done." Sam and Freddie both nodded. "Good. Let's get to work."

Freddie stood as well. "Right!"

But Sam yawned. "Ah, you guys start." She headed for the stairs. "I'm gonna go take a nap."

A few nights later, Carly stood in the middle of their studio. She was wearing a yellow and pink sleeveless cheerleading outfit and carrying matching pom-poms. Her hair was done up in pigtails with pink ribbons. A pink heart adorned the front of her uniform, and a matching necklace hung just above it. The green screen behind her was programmed to have an animated sequence of rotating planets.

"And now," Freddie announced as he filmed, "the adventures of Melanie Higgles" — Carly leaped into the scene, doing her best "peppy cheerleader" stance — "space cheerleader!"

"Oh, yeah, uh-huh, oh, yeah! Weeee!" Carly performed a little cheer.

Then a squeaking noise distracted her as Sam rode into the picture on a big tricycle. She was wearing a cheerleading outfit as well, but hers was all black and dark red. A demon decorated the front.

"Melanie Higgles," Sam intoned in a deep voice, getting off the tricycle.

"Oh, yeah!" Carly replied. "Uh-huh! What's up, what's up, what's up?!"

"Come to the dark side of space cheerleading," Sam instructed her.

Carly did a little frown and then a pout. "No way! Get 'outer' my space!" She grinned at the camera. "Oh, yeah!"

"Come to the dark side," Sam repeated. Carly refused again, and Sam growled at her. Carly growled back. Then they produced oversized padded clubs and began beating each other with them, doing little cheers the whole time.

"And—we're clear!" Freddie told them, ending the feed.

Carly immediately dropped the cheerleader act. "So, what'd you think?"

"Hilarious!" Freddie was still laughing. "It's awesome!"

Sam smiled. "See?" she told Carly.

Carly nodded. "We've got our bit for the iWeb Awards."

"Yeah we do!" Sam held up her fist, and she and Carly fist-bumped. "So what's next?"

Freddie crossed to his laptop. "Well, if you guys are interested, I went online and found all kinds of interesting facts about Japan."

"Really? Well, tell us!" Carly demanded. But she and Sam were already walking to the elevator. They asked Freddie a whole bunch of questions, getting into the elevator and heading down the whole time. They didn't stop until the doors had closed in front of them.

Sometimes messing with Freddie was way too easy. And way too much fun!

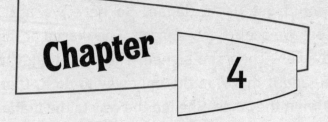

Chapter 4

"Tell me again why we're not on a regular plane?" Carly asked. They were standing on the runway staring at the airplane in front of them. At least, she thought it was an airplane. It had a long thick body and big wide wings with heavy propellers and a tail at one end. But most of the planes she'd seen before were sleek and colorful. This thing was big and ugly and battered and drab. It looked like a slug with wings.

"This was the best Socko could do," Spencer explained again, hefting some of their luggage.

"And why did Socko have anything to do with our travel arrangements?" Socko was Spencer's best friend. A travel agent, he was not. He sold socks for a living.

"I couldn't exchange the tickets," Spencer admitted. "They were the kind that, well, that you can't exchange. But Socko said he knew a guy

31

who could get us to Japan. So here we are!"

"Here we are!" Carly agreed. She stared at the plane again. Then she sighed. They had to get to Japan, and if this was the only way to do it, then that's what they'd do. She led the way to the plane.

"Well, howdy!" A man shouted as they approached. He was as stout and grubby as the plane. He wore a beaten-up leather jacket over a stained white T-shirt and dirty chinos tucked into heavy, scuffed work boots. A grimy baseball cap was pulled down over short greasy hair, and he was chewing on what looked like a short, stout cigar. He had a big grin on his face. "I'm Freight Dog," he announced. "You're Socko's pals?"

"That's right!" Spencer matched the man's enthusiasm. "I'm Spencer; this is my sister, Carly; and that's Freddie; his mom, Mrs. Benson; and Sam." Everyone nodded hello — their hands were too full to wave.

"Well, okay then! Let's go — time's a-wastin'!" He led them up to an open hatch along the side of the plane, hopped up the short set of metal stairs, and stepped through. Spencer had to duck to follow.

"C'mon, this way," Freight Dog encouraged them, leading them back through the plane. There were boxes piled high on both sides, leaving only a narrow aisle. No, not boxes, Carly realized as something yipped at her. Cages. They were all animal cages. And at least some of them were full of, well, animals.

"Keep a'comin'," Freight Dog urged them. "Oh, watch where you step!" He hadn't made any effort to help them with their bags.

"So, your name is Freight Dog?" Spencer asked.

"Yep!" Freight Dog replied. He pulled the cigar out of his mouth and waved it in Spencer's face. "And this is my pepperoni!" He was right, Carly noticed. It wasn't a cigar at all — it was part of a whole pepperoni. Maybe he liked to snack while he flew?

"Well, thanks for letting me smell it," Spencer told him, trying to put some room between them without stepping on Carly.

"This is your airplane?" Carly asked the man.

"Yep!" He looked pretty pleased with himself.

Sam glanced around behind Carly. "Wow,"

she commented. "This is almost as nice as a gas station men's room."

Freight Dog beamed at her. "Thanks!"

They were now at the very back of the plane, where the space widened out enough that they could at least all stand clustered together. Carly noticed the cages around them were marked LIVE POSSOM. Sure enough, each one contained at least one of the fuzzy little animals.

"Um, what are all these possums for?" she asked.

Freight Dog looked around. "That's my cargo on this trip," he explained. "Anything anybody wants transported overseas, I fly it."

Mrs. Benson looked like she was going to be sick. "Are the possums safe?" she asked hesitantly, clutching Freddie protectively.

Freight Dog studied her for a second. "No, ma'am," he admitted, "they're fulla disease." Then he grinned at all of them. "Okay! Let's fly!"

Mrs. Benson looked like she was going to throw up.

"Wait. Uh." Freddie raised his hand. "Where's the restroom on this plane?"

"Oh, here ya go." Freight Dog tossed Freddie a rusty metal bucket. "If you guys fill that one up, I got more buckets in back," he assured them.

"Excuse me!" Mrs. Benson took the bucket from Freddie and stepped forward. "I am not going to do my 'business' in this bucket. I am a lady." Carly noticed she didn't say anything about the idea of Freddie — or the rest of them — having to use it.

Freight Dog actually looked a little apologetic. "Oh right, sorry." He turned and reached behind him again. "Here." The new bucket he shoved at her was just like the first one, except that it had been painted pink and had flower stickers all over it. Mrs. Benson took it reflexively, and by the time she opened her mouth to say anything else Freight Dog had tossed the other bucket back to Freddie, given him a big thumbs-up, and vanished back down the narrow corridor. A minute later they heard the plane's engines rumble to life.

"I can't believe this is how we're getting to Japan," Sam muttered as they all dropped their luggage and cleared off a row of wooden crates so they could sit down.

"It could be worse," Carly offered, pounding her backpack a little to try and make it more comfortable behind her back.

"Yeah? How?"

Carly thought about that for a second. "We could be sharing the flight with that French guy and his puppet," she offered finally.

Sam considered that. "Point," she finally admitted. Then the plane lurched forward, almost knocking her to the floor — Carly wasn't too happy about even her feet touching that surface. "Though at least they looked soft," Sam muttered.

Carly just nodded. There wasn't much else to say, and with the rumbling all around them no one would have heard her anyway.

"This is insane," Carly said out loud. They had been in the air for hours. At least the shuddering and shaking had smoothed out a little once they'd left the ground. The noise was still just as bad, though, and their makeshift seats just as uncomfortable. And the facilities — she watched Sam return from farther down the corridor and hang the pink bucket back on a nail in the wall. She shuddered. Best not to think about it.

"I know," Freddie agreed. He was sitting next to her, of course. "I can't believe I'm flying to Japan on a cargo plane surrounded by possi."

"Huh?" Carly wasn't sure she'd heard him correctly. "Possi?"

"What is 'possi'?" Sam asked, dropping down on Carly's other side.

"It's the plural of 'possum,'" Freddie told them.

Carly chuckled. "No it's not."

Freddie nodded. "One possum. Many possi."

That got a snort out of Sam. "That's so stupid," she pronounced. One thing Sam was certainly good at was making definitive statements. No wishy-washiness in her!

Freddie glared at her. "It is not!"

"Whatever." Sam threw up her hands, rose to her feet again, and walked over to the far side of the hold. Not that she was able to go very far.

The plane hit an air pocket and everyone gasped. "I'm having anxiety," Mrs. Benson suddenly announced. She was sitting in the far corner and rocking back and forth, her purse clutched protectively in front of her.

Spencer was sitting next to her and glanced around to see who she was talking to. "Okay," he replied finally. She didn't seem to want or need any other answer, so he went quiet again.

"Are you cold?" Freddie asked Carly suddenly.

She shivered. "Little bit," she admitted. There didn't seem to be any heat on this plane — not that she should be surprised by that, really, given its equal lack of plumbing.

"Maybe we should snuggle close together," Freddie suggested slowly. "You know, to keep warm and —"

Carly cut him off. "No."

"All right," Freddie agreed. He knew there was no point in arguing.

"Hey," Sam called over to them. She'd wandered over to a stack of possum cages and had opened one — now she had the possum cradled in her arms like a baby. "Look at me with a possum!" She petted it a little. It was actually kind of cute.

But Carly didn't think Sam had claimed the animal for its cuteness. "Sam, don't eat him!" she warned.

Sam rolled her eyes. "I'm not gonna"—she paused and considered the animal in her arms for a second before continuing—"I'm not gonna eat him." That was a first—Sam would eat almost anything. Literally. Carly figured the only reason Sam didn't eat rocks was because they were too hard on her teeth.

"Sam, be careful with that thing," Mrs. Benson added. "You don't know where it's been!"

Freddie laughed at his mom's warning. "Like we know where Sam's been?" he asked. Sam glared at him in reply—but she put the possum back in its cage. She had just closed its door again when Freight Dog emerged from the corridor to the cockpit. He had a thick rope over his shoulder.

"How's everybody doin'?" he asked.

They all stared at him. "Shouldn't you be flying the plane?" Carly asked.

"What do you think this rope's for?" he answered. "See?" He gave it a hard tug and

39

everyone else screamed as the plane suddenly lurched to one side. They all shouted at him and after a second he relaxed the rope again, letting the plane level out.

Sam had somehow managed to stay on her feet. "Hey, why are you taking all these possums to Japan, anyway?" she asked.

Freight Dog laughed. "Oh, they're not going to Japan," he answered. "They're going to Korea. Possi are the most popular pets there now." Freddie looked triumphant at the use of the word "possi," but the others just stared.

Spencer found his voice first. "But wait —" he got up and stepped over to Freight Dog. "Socko said you're taking us to Japan."

"No," Freight Dog corrected. "I'm takin' ya *over* Japan. Here, hold my pepperoni!" he thrust it at Spencer.

"Oh, may I?" Spencer retorted. He took the thing, but dumped it in the pink bucket the minute Freight Dog turned away. Carly was busy watching Freight Dog as he approached the far wall and the heavy door set into it. He flipped a lever and pushed the door open. Winds gusted into the cargo hold, knocking all of them about.

"Welcome to Japan!" Freight Dog shouted. He checked his watch. "We should be over Tokyo in about five minutes. That's when you jump!" He stepped over to a nearby crate and lifted the lid, revealing a row of what looked like big heavy backpacks. "I recommend using a parachute," he continued, pulling one out. "Who wants one?"

Freight Dog started tossing parachutes to everyone. Then he pulled goggles from a smaller crate and distributed those as well. Everyone took them. They were too stunned to speak.

Finally Carly managed to swallow. "We're parachuting into Japan?" she asked no one in particular. Freight Dog nodded, though. Carly looked past him, out the open door, and gulped. She could feel her stomach start to bubble. "Can someone hand me the pink bucket?" she demanded.

"If you guys wanna land in Tokyo," Freight Dog advised a few minutes later, "you better jump in the next two minutes!" He headed back to the cockpit. Apparently the rope had its limits.

Carly and the others stared at each other. They'd all buckled on their parachutes and donned their goggles — all except Mrs. Benson. She had hers clutched in front of her in a death grip.

"I am not putting on this parachute," she insisted desperately. "I would rather go to Korea with the diseased possi."

Carly turned to Spencer. "How can your friend Socko not have mentioned that we'd have to jump out of the plane into Japan?" she demanded.

Spencer looked like he always did when he'd done something foolish — which was most of the time. "He might have mentioned it," he admitted, having to shout to be heard over the wind. "He said Freight Dog could 'drop us' in Japan. I didn't realize he actually meant *drop* us!"

Sam pushed her way up next to them and the open door. "We gotta get to the iWeb Awards," she pointed out, "so let's just jump."

Freddie joined them. "Guys, there's no way my mom's jumping outta this airplane," he warned.

They all glanced over at Mrs. Benson, who was now cowering in the corner.

"I know how to make her jump," Sam assured him.

Freddie shook his head. "No chance. She's been afraid of heights ever since —"

He didn't get to finish his sentence, because Sam suddenly hip-checked him — right out the open door! Carly was shocked — even for Sam that was extreme!

Freddie screamed as he disappeared from view, and Mrs. Benson leaped forward, tugging her parachute on as she barreled toward them. "I'm coming, Freddie!" she shouted as she dove headfirst out of the plane. "*Pechangaaaaaahh!*"

Carly, Sam, and Spencer stood there for a second, watching her go. "Okay," Carly said finally. "Who's next?"

Her brother gulped. "Ladies first," he insisted.

"All right, fine." Carly pulled on her goggles and turned to Sam. "Hold my hand?" she pleaded. They locked hands.

"Ready?" Sam asked her. She looked a little bit scared, too, which made Carly worry even

more. Nothing scared Sam! Well, nothing normal.

"Shouldn't we count to three first?" Carly objected. But Sam shook her head.

"Nope! Just scream!"

Carly gulped but nodded. "When?"

"Now!" Sam screamed and leaped forward, and Carly jumped quickly to stay with her. The winds tore at them, and Carly could barely breathe. She was glad for the goggles, and for Sam's hand clenched in hers, and for the heavy weight of the parachute across her back. They plummeted through several layers of filmy clouds and then the ground rushed into view. It was coming up fast!

All at once Sam yanked on her arm. Carly glanced over and saw that her best friend had her free hand on her parachute's pull cord. Carly quickly grasped her own and nodded. They tugged at the same time, and both screamed again as their parachutes burst open, yanking them suddenly upward and pulling them apart. After a few seconds they both began descending again, but now it was a much slower, gentler drop. Carly glanced around and smiled. She could see the Japanese countryside spread out before her. It was really pretty.

"Get ready!" Sam shouted over to her suddenly. Carly glanced down and realized the ground was right below them! She bent her knees and a second later they hit the ground, but the parachute made it no worse than jumping off a short ladder. Carly rolled with the impact, then straightened up and shrugged out of the parachute straps. Sam was right behind her, and Carly quickly jogged over to her best friend.

"Whoa," Carly managed. Her legs were a little wobbly from the landing, and she was gasping for air, but she felt great.

"That was insane!" Sam agreed next to her.

"I know!"

"We're in Japan!"

"I know!" Carly repeated.

Sam was already looking around. "Where's a sushi bar?" she wanted to know. All that action had made her hungry.

Just then they heard a strangled sound behind them. It was Mrs. Benson. *"Ulch!"* she complained.

"I can't get out of this psychotic parachute!" Freddie was trying to help her, and Carly was glad to see he'd made it down safely as well. After a minute he managed to get his mom free of the straps, and she threw it away from her as hard as she could.

"Stupid thing!" she shouted at the poor parachute. "I can't believe we were forced to jump into Japan! When I see Spencer I am going to tell him in no uncertain terms that I —"

Just then Carly heard Spencer shout from up above, "Here I come!" The next second he glided down toward them — but he was too close and he slammed full-force into Mrs. Benson, knocking her to the ground.

"Mom!" Freddie shouted, rushing to her side as Spencer landed and rolled to a stop. Carly and Sam ran over to help him up.

"You all right?" Carly asked her brother. Behind her, Freddie was asking his mom the same question.

"Yeah!" Spencer answered as they pulled him to his feet. "Whoa!" he burst out laughing. "That was intense!"

Freddie stepped over beside them. "I think Freight Dog threw our luggage outta the plane," he announced, glancing up at the sky.

"What makes you think that?" Carly asked him. She had her answer an instant later, as it began raining luggage. Freight Dog hadn't bothered to equip the bags and suitcases with parachutes, and they hit the ground with heavy thuds — all except the ones that splashed into a nearby pond.

Sam rushed to her suitcase, which had just landed, and opened it up. "Yes!" she pulled a snack out and held it high. "The Fat Cakes are okay!" she announced.

Freddie was still looking around. "Hey, did anybody see my red backpack come down?"

They all scanned the area for it. Then Mrs. Benson cried out. Freddie's red backpack had just come down on her head! She fell to the ground again.

Carly counted the luggage she could see, including the ones in the water. "Okay, I think that's everything," she told the others. Mrs. Benson was moaning and asking what had happened — the red bag had taken her by surprise!

"I'll go get those," Spencer offered, shucking his parachute and wading into the pond to retrieve the pieces there. Unfortunately most of their luggage wasn't waterproof. Carly hoped nothing important was in those bags.

They were gathering everything together when Sam asked an important question.

"So where are we, exactly?"

Carly glanced around and realized Sam was right. It looked like they were out in the middle of a field. It clearly wasn't downtown Tokyo!

"Yeah, and how are we going to get to Tokyo?" she added, letting out a groan. They'd only been in the country a few minutes, and they were *already* lost in the middle of nowhere. Couldn't anything about this trip go right?

"I guess we walk," Sam replied.

"Makes sense," Freddie agreed. "Just one problem — which direction?"

Carly groaned again.

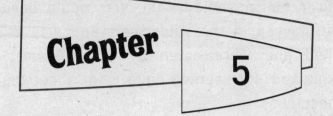

Chapter 5

"Finally," Carly said as they staggered into the Hotel Nakamura's front lobby several hours later. It was beautiful, with smooth bamboo floors, curved door arches, elegant carved columns that glowed from within, and a long rectangular pond running against the far wall.

"The front desk is right over there," Officer Makai informed her, gesturing across the elegant lobby to the long curving desk. He had offered to drive them to the hotel after he'd spotted them staggering about in the rice fields. Carly suspected it was just to make sure they didn't trample any more crops.

"Thank you so much," Carly told him, and the others all chimed in as well.

"I don't know what we would've done if you hadn't found us," Spencer added.

Officer Makai smiled. "Oh, you would have slowly starved in the wilderness until you all perished and were eaten by wild animals," he explained. He seemed quite calm about the prospect.

Spencer nodded slowly. "Right."

"Well, thanks so much," Carly repeated. What else could she say to something like that?

Officer Makai bowed and said something in response — it was in Japanese, but Carly suspected it meant "you're welcome." Then he straightened, placed his cap back on his head, saluted them, and walked out.

"He was nice," Freddie commented.

"He was weird," Carly corrected.

Sam grinned. "I took his handcuffs." She held them up for everyone to see. *Right,* Carly corrected in her head — Sam *was weird.* Compared to her, Officer Makai seemed perfectly normal.

"I'll go check us in," Spencer announced after a second.

That got a groan from Mrs. Benson, who had sunk down onto one of the lobby's many couches. "Haven't you done enough?" she demanded.

"I'll do it," Carly said quickly. She just wanted to avoid any more arguments and get them into their rooms as soon as possible.

"I'll go with you," Freddie offered. The two of them walked over to the front desk and stepped up to an available clerk, an attractive young Japanese lady wearing a red silk shirt.

"Hello, welcome to Hotel Nakamura," she told them. "May I help you?"

"Yeah, we're checking in," Carly replied. She and Freddie shared a smile. It felt so grown-up to say that!

Apparently the hotel clerk thought they were grown-up, too! "*Ohhh*, honeymoon couple!" she cooed.

Freddie grinned at Carly—right up until she slapped him. Gently. Just hard enough to wipe that expression off his face.

"No," she corrected the clerk. "My name's Carly Shay. We have reservations through the iWeb Awards."

The clerk checked her computer screen. "Yes," she confirmed after a second or two. "Let me check and see what room you are in."

Just then a paunchy man with a silly black beret rushed up to the desk and shoved past Carly to speak to the clerk. He had a pink poodle puppet on his left hand. Carly recognized him at once. It was Henri P'Twa and his puppet Oompé — their competitors for the Best Web Comedy award!

"Zees is a catastrophe!" Henri announced to the clerk in a weird French accent. "You must talk wiz me now!"

"Excuse me," Freddie, interrupted, "but we were here first." He was polite but firm about it. Not that it mattered much.

"*Fermez la bouche*!" Henri snapped at him — Carly suspected that Henri was telling them to shut up. He shoved the puppet in Freddie's face, silencing him. Then he turned to the clerk again. "I was supposed to have a separate room for my poopit," he insisted haughtily.

"Your poopit?" The clerk looked confused. Carly couldn't blame her.

"What's a poopit?" Carly asked.

"Poopit!" Henri repeated, waving Oompé in their faces.

Freddie stared at it. "Puppet?" he corrected. Oompé growled at Freddie. "Okay . . ."

Carly was starting to get a little annoyed. "Look," she told the Frenchman, "I've had a really tough day which included jumping out of a cargo plane full of possums and wandering in the Japanese wilderness for seven hours, so I'd —" But Henri had already turned his back on her!

"I cannot share a room wiz zees poopit!" Henri informed the clerk again, completely ignoring Carly and Freddie.

"Sir—" Carly tried again, but a hand on her arm stopped her.

It was Sam. "I got this," she assured them. Sam stepped in, yanked the puppet off Henri's hand, and hurled it as hard as she could across the lobby. Oompé sailed off in a streak of pink fluff.

Henri shrieked. "Oompé!" Then he raced off after his beloved puppet.

"Can I please check in?" Carly begged the clerk. The woman looked amused by the recent puppet departure and nodded pleasantly.

"Yes, the iWeb Awards have provided you with a double suite," she replied. She typed in a few commands and pulled several key cards out of a machine to one side, inserting them in a small folder and offering them to Carly. "I hope you find the rooms to your liking."

"Thanks." Carly took the folder and headed back over to Spencer and Mrs. Benson, Sam and Freddie right behind her. "'Kay, we're all set," she told them.

Spencer hopped up from the couch, a smile on his face. "Awesome!"

"Finally!" Mrs. Benson took a little bit more effort to rise to her feet. They all grabbed their luggage and traipsed off toward the elevators.

"Ah, enjoy your honeymoon!" the clerk called out to Carly as they passed the front desk.

"Stop saying that!" Carly shouted back. Then she had to slap Freddie again. A little harder this time.

"This is so exciting!" Spencer blurted out as the bellman showed them to their rooms, which were large, handsome, and understated. "My first pee in a foreign country!"

"Have fun," Carly told him. She couldn't help

laughing. She loved her brother dearly, but he was a complete and utter goofball most of the time. Still, he was *her* complete and utter goofball brother, and she knew he was always there for her. That meant a lot.

Sam dropped her bags by the bed on the far side of the room and let out an enormous yawn. "I gotta crash," she mumbled.

Carly nodded. "Me, too." She was exhausted. They all were.

Mrs. Benson came back into the room — she'd wandered into the other one to check it out. Carly was assuming both of them had two double beds — she and Sam had already planned to share one. "So," Mrs. Benson said brightly, "how are we going to split up? Maybe the boys in this room and us girls in the other?"

Carly and Sam exchanged a quick glance, sudden horror making them super-alert. "No!" they blurted out together. Sharing a room with Mrs. Benson? What a nightmare!

"Wouldn't you rather share a room with your sweet son, Freddie?" Carly suggested. She felt terrible about selling Freddie out like this, but

Mrs. Benson was *his* mom. And the idea of Mrs. Benson in their room? Definitely bad.

Sam walked over to Mrs. Benson and touched her gently on one arm. "Freddie needs you," was all she said. Sometimes, Carly thought, Sam was brilliant.

Freddie was less appreciative. "Guys!"

But his mom had already turned to him. "No, Freddie, they're right," she agreed. She picked up her suitcase and headed for the adjoining room.

"Thanks a lot," Freddie snapped at the girls before following her. Carly did feel bad about it — Freddie had to put up with his overprotective mom all the time at home, and she'd just made it so he had to deal with her here as well. But better him than her. Sam simply stuck out her tongue — she obviously wasn't as concerned.

Now it was just the two of them in their room. "Hey, where'd Spencer go?" she asked.

"In here!" her brother called out. He emerged from the bathroom a second later, holding something in his hand. "Look, they leave you these cute little candies in the bathroom!" He popped it into his mouth. "I am lovin' this hotel! Did you

guys know they have twenty-four hour room—"
Suddenly his face contorted into a horrible
grimace. "It's soap," he gasped. He spit the soap
out into his hand. Then he coughed—and a
soap bubble burst from his mouth. Spencer stared
as it floated in front of him for a second before
popping.

"Look at it this way," Sam consoled him. "You
can go to sleep with your mouth all nice and
clean!"

"Hey, yeah!" Spencer blew another soap bubble. Carly shook her head and brushed past him
for the bathroom to wash up and get ready for
bed. She wasn't going to eat any soap, though,
she decided. She'd leave that fun for Spencer and
content herself with cleaning her mouth the old-
fashioned way—with toothpaste.

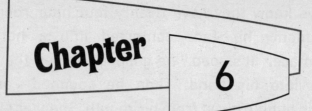

Chapter 6

Knock, knock!

Carly struggled to wake herself. What was that?

Beside her, Sam stirred. "Carly," she muttered, "someone's knockin' at the door."

"Uh-huh," Carly agreed foggily.

Freddie stumbled into their room. "Someone's knocking," he reported. He made no move to answer it, however. Neither did anybody else. The knocking continued.

Carly groaned and hauled herself out of bed. "I'll get it," she mumbled. As she passed the other bed, where her brother was sprawled out, she couldn't resist tickling his exposed feet. "Wake up!" she told him. He giggled and started to wake.

"Who is it?" Carly asked through the door.

"Kyoko and Yuki," a girl answered.

iGo to Japan

Freddie hard at work on *iCarly*.

Don't ever ask Sam for pudding. She might throw it right in your face!

Melanie Higgles! Space Cheerleader!

Battling evil cheerleaders across the galaxy!

Riding to Tokyo in a plane full of possums was *not* fun!

But jumping out of the plane was
kind of awesome!

Our competition: Kyoko and Yuki

Freddie filmed as much of Tokyo as he could—even the boring parts.

Ms. Benson got all wrapped up in seaweed—just like a piece of sushi!

Spencer and Ms. Benson used the tracking chip in Freddie's head to find us.

We had trouble fitting everyone in our tiny Japanese cab.

We didn't have our nominee badges so the security guards wouldn't let us into the iWeb Awards. So unfair!

Kyoko and Yuki were pretty funny—even if they were cheaters.

Freddie tapped into the big screen and shared a video of me and Sam during Kyoko and Yuki's performance. **Take that, cheaters!**

They finally brought us onstage and the crowd went nuts. **They loved us!**

We won the iWeb Awards!
Go *iCarly*!

Carly peered through the peephole. There was a Japanese boy and girl on the other side. He was tall and had spiky hair, she was short and had her hair in pigtails. He was also carrying a large gift basket. Carly recognized them at once from the iWeb nominee videos, but it still took her brain a second to process. "Kyoko and Yuki?" she repeated.

"Our competition?" Sam asked. She'd now stumbled out of bed as well.

"Who are Kyoko and Yuki?" Spencer asked.

"Uh, the kids who star in one of the Web shows we're competing against," Freddie told him.

"What are they doin' here?" Sam wanted to know.

Carly shrugged. Only one way to find out! She opened the door. "Hi!"

The boy spoke first. "Hello, I am Yuki."

"Kyoko," the girl introduced herself. "Welcome to Japan." Yuki enthusiastically seconded her greeting.

"Thanks!" Carly blinked. "Come on in." She'd been worried that everyone would be all competitive about the awards, but Kyoko and Yuki seemed really nice.

Sam and Freddie said hi as the kids entered, and Carly introduced all of them, but Kyoko and Yuki waved aside the introductions.

"We love your Web show," Kyoko explained. Yuki nodded and beamed beside her.

"Hey, we love yours," Freddie responded. Carly and Sam agreed.

"Oh, and this is my brother, Spencer," Carly added as he rolled out of bed.

Spencer said something in Japanese, and Yuki and Kyoko responded enthusiastically. But then he looked confused. Carly was guessing his Japanese language lessons hadn't gotten very far — it would explain why his neck still had burn marks. "I ate soap," he finally answered in English.

Kyoko and Yuki looked confused, and Carly hastened to explain their fuzziness and their attire. "We just woke up."

Yuki laughed. "At three o'clock in the afternoon?"

That surprised them! Carly glanced at the clock on the bedside table. Sure enough, it said 3:12 P.M. It must have been the jet lag!

Sam wasn't very happy about this. "We slept through breakfast and lunch?" she shouted.

"Shh, shh," Carly consoled her. She grabbed one of Sam's snacks from her open suitcase and handed it to her. "Fat Cake." Sam tore into it.

"What are you guys doing here?" Carly asked once she was sure Sam wouldn't try to bite anyone.

"Well, we found out that you were staying at this hotel—" Kyoko started to answer,

"—and we wanted to welcome you to Tokyo," Yuki finished. It was like they'd rehearsed the line. Then Kyoko took the gift basket from Yuki and offered it to Carly. "Please accept this expensive gift basket."

"*Aww*, thanks." Carly took it. She was thrilled—who knew they'd find new friends here?

"So, your trip here was good?" Yuki asked as Carly set the basket on the table.

Carly nodded. "Yeah, the plane ride was pretty insane."

"Till we had to jump out," Sam added.

Kyoko looked surprised. "You jumped out of your airplane?"

"Some jumped," Freddie corrected. He glared at Sam. "Some were pushed." She actually looked away. Carly wondered if this was one of those rare occasions where Sam felt bad about something she'd done to Freddie. But probably not.

"We know it sounds weird—" Carly agreed. She thought about it. "Cuz, well, it was weird. But we're fine."

"We are. Some of our luggage fell to its death," Sam pointed out.

Freddie sighed. "Drowned in a lake."

Spencer was still stuck on his earlier mistake. "I thought the soap was candy," he told Kyoko again. She and Yuki both stared at Spencer.

"Well," Kyoko said finally, "if some of your luggage 'drowned' as you say—"

"—would you like us to take you shopping?" Yuki finished. It was eerie the way they did that! But Carly was focusing on that last word.

"Shopping?" she repeated eagerly. She loved to shop! And she'd never shopped in a foreign country before!

Freddie was practical, as always. "Do we have time?" he asked.

"Oh yes," Kyoko assured him. "The iWeb Awards do not start for five hours."

"Plenty of time," Yuki agreed.

Just then Mrs. Benson wandered in. She was wearing a lovely Japanese robe and holding another one. "Freddie," she called out, "Freddie, look at these wonderful robes the hotel gives you." Then she noticed Kyoko and Yuki. "Oh, hello," she said, pulling her robe closed more tightly. "Could we get a few extra towels and some unscented toilet paper?" She pronounced each word slowly and carefully.

Sam sighed. "They don't work here, crazy," she told Freddie's mom.

"They have a Web show that got nominated for an iWeb award," Freddie explained quickly.

"It's a pleasure to meet you," Kyoko said. She and Yuki shook Mrs. Benson's hand.

"They want to take us shopping!" Carly burst out.

"Ooo, I'd like to go shopping," Mrs. Benson agreed, which quickly dampened some of

63

Carly's enthusiasm. Kyoko and Yuki exchanged a look — they didn't seem too happy about that idea, either. But they smiled.

"Oh, well, we would love for you to join us," Yuki assured her.

Kyoko nodded. "But for the grown-ups," she added, "Yuki and I have arranged traditional Japanese seaweed massages."

That got Spencer's attention. "Massages?"

Mrs. Benson was clearly interested as well. "Oh, I could use a good rubbing," she announced, which was an image Carly had never wanted in her mind and hoped would go away soon.

"Here." Yuki handed Spencer and Mrs. Benson what looked like two certificates, except they were covered in beautiful Japanese writing. "Our cousins work at the spa just down the street. You will have a wonderful massage there." Spencer and Mrs. Benson bowed and thanked them.

Then Kyoko turned to Carly, Sam, and Freddie. "So, shall we go shopping?"

Carly grinned, excited again. "Sure, just give us a little time to shower and get dressed?"

Yuki bowed. "Of course."

"Freddie," Mrs. Benson instructed, "make sure you put on a fresh pair of anti-bacterial underpants."

"Mom!" Freddie looked mortified. Everyone else tried not to laugh — except for Sam, who never bothered to hide her amusement at anything that made Freddie uncomfortable.

"We will meet you in the lobby," Kyoko told them as she and Yuki headed for the door.

"Great! We'll be right down!" Carly waited until the door had closed before squealing with Sam. "We're going shopping! In Japan!"

"I know!" Sam shouted back. Then she spied the gift basket. "Hey, food!"

Carly left her to open and devour the basket's contents while she washed up and got dressed. She just hoped Sam didn't eat the actual basket before she got back.

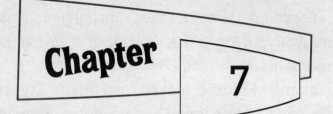

Chapter 7

Several hours later, the thrill was gone. And so was their time.

"We are heading back to the hotel, right?" Carly asked again.

"Cuz it looks like we're in the middle of nowhere," Sam chimed in beside her. The three of them were in the back seat of Yuki's minivan, while Kyoko and Yuki were up front. The pair had spent the past few hours arguing, half in English and half in Japanese, about which way to go. Eventually, Yuki had admitted that he must have missed a turn, and had claimed he was taking them back to their hotel, but it was nowhere in sight. Carly was pretty sure they weren't even in the city anymore. In fact, she could have sworn they'd just passed the spot where they'd jumped from the plane — she'd thought she'd seen an abandoned parachute, but it was dark out now so she couldn't be sure.

Sam had been annoyed at the delays — and at the lack of food. Freddie had been annoyed as well, but was contenting himself with filming everything on his portable digital video camera — which shot in high-def, he'd pointed out when Sam had teased him about it. But Carly, stuck in the middle as usual, wasn't entertained. She was just worried.

Up front, Yuki sighed and shook his head. "Okay, we're lost."

"I knew it!" Kyoko declared. She twisted in her seat to look back at Carly and the others. "I am sorry we spoiled your welcome to our country."

Carly tried to put a cheerful face on things. "Oh, c'mon, you didn't spoil our welcome," she claimed.

Just then the van's engine sputtered. They rolled to a stop along the side of the road. There was nothing around but a few trees, some scrub brush, and the darkness.

Freddie lowered his camera and leaned forward. "Uhh, why did we stop?"

Yuki banged on the steering wheel. "We're out of gas," he admitted.

Carly, Sam, and Freddie looked at each other.

Carly shook her head, her attempts at optimism defeated. "And now the welcome is spoiled."

Kyoko turned to Yuki. "You didn't get gas?" she accused.

"Yes, I got gas!" he replied angrily. "Then we drove very far in the wrong direction and now gas is gone!"

Freddie was checking his watch. The news wasn't good. "And the iWeb Awards start in an hour and a half."

As usual, Sam put things in perspective. "Well, ain't this sweet," she declared. "The five of us are gonna miss the Awards, so Frenchie and his 'poopit' are gonna win Best Comedy Show on the Web." Everyone groaned at the thought.

"Can't you guys just call your parents or someone to come pick us up?" Freddie asked.

"We don't have cell phones with us," Kyoko admitted sadly. Which was weird because Carly had thought she'd seen Yuki checking one earlier on the drive. But it must have been an MP3 player or something.

Fortunately, she never went anywhere without her phone! "Okay," she said, whipping it out, "then I'll just call Spencer so —"

But Yuki shook his head. "Your American cell phones don't work in Japan," he explained. Oh.

Kyoko was furious. "You have ruined everything!" she informed her partner. "I told you when to turn but you refused!"

Yuki glared at her. "What about the time you left my bicycle out in the rain?" he shouted.

Kyoko looked as confused as Carly felt. "That was nine years ago!"

Yuki frowned and crossed his arms. "I'm still upset!"

These two were weird!

Then Kyoko and Yuki started yelling at each other in Japanese. Carly had no idea what they were saying, but it sure didn't sound happy.

"This is bad," she told Sam and Freddie. Freddie nodded — but Sam was laughing!

Carly couldn't believe it. "This is serious!" she insisted. "Why are you laughing?"

Sam shook her head. She was still laughing. "Somethin' about Japanese arguing cracks me up," she explained.

Up front, Yuki yelled something and Kyoko gasped. That couldn't be good. Then she grabbed her water bottle from the cup holder beside her and squirted water in Yuki's face, which made him gasp in return. No, definitely not good. The next thing Carly knew, the Japanese duo were clambering out of the van.

"They're leaving the van," she told Freddie and Sam, as if they couldn't see for themselves. "Why are they leaving the van?"

Freddie craned his neck to look behind them. "They're fighting!" he reported.

"What?" Carly pushed Freddie against the door and, taking her hint, he quickly opened it and scrambled outside. Sam was already out the other door — she never needed an excuse to watch a good fight.

Sure enough, Kyoko and Yuki were trading kicks and punches on the road a little way behind the van. This was Japan, though, so it was all martial arts. It was like watching a Jackie Chan movie, Carly thought, only in real life!

Sam was loving it, of course. "Hey." She nudged Freddie, "Gimme your camcorder." Freddie handed it over without a word, and Sam started filming Kyoko and Yuki.

"Why are you recording this?" Carly wanted to know.

"To put on iCarly-dot-com," Sam replied without lowering the camera. "Kids love violence."

Yuki kicked out, just missing Kyoko but making her stumble backward. He was right behind her, and somehow spun her around to trap her in a headlock, but a second later she twisted to one side and flipped him on his back.

"C'mon, Yuki!" Sam suddenly shouted. "Get up and show her what your foot tastes like!" As if taking her advice to heart, Yuki sprang to his feet again and traded another series of quick blows with Kyoko. Sam continued to cheer, though she kept switching who she was rooting for.

Carly hoped her brother and Freddie's mom were having a good time. Somebody should!

☺ ☺ ☺ ☺ ☺

Unfortunately, things weren't going that well for Spencer and Mrs. Benson either.

It had started off well enough. They had gone to the massage parlor and presented the certificates Kyoko and Yuki had given them. The masseurs had been very nice and had taken them to changing rooms, where they both were given robes to wear — and nothing else! Then they'd been led to a room with two massage tables. Spencer and Mrs. Benson had been told to lie down, and the masseurs had removed their robes and wrapped them in seaweed.

The masseurs told them to relax and headed toward the door. Spencer asked when they'd be unwrapped, and one of the masseurs paused long enough to answer, "When the iWeb Awards are over — after Kyoko and Yuki have won!" Then they left the room and locked the door behind them.

"We've been set up!" Mrs. Benson gasped.

"Yeah," Spencer agreed. "I don't think those Kyoko and Yuki kids are as nice as they seemed."

That got another gasp from Mrs. Benson. "The children! We have to warn them!"

"Relax," Spencer told her. "This is just seaweed — how strong can it be?"

Unfortunately, the answer proved to be — plenty strong! Spencer's attempts to break free only resulted in tipping his whole table over. He wound up on the floor, still wrapped tight.

But then he had an idea. "Seaweed is edible," he recalled. "If I can't break my way out, maybe I can eat my way out!" Spencer started chewing, tearing hunks of seaweed off with his teeth. He told Mrs. Benson to try with hers, but she couldn't reach.

"We Bensons have short necks," she explained with a sigh.

"Well, don't worry," Spencer told her through a mouthful of seaweed. "I'm gonna have us outta here fast!"

It took a while, but eventually he managed to break free from his seaweed binding. Mrs. Benson wanted him to chew her out next, but Spencer told her he couldn't. "I'm full," he claimed. Fortunately, there was a Japanese sword hanging on the wall, so he used that to cut her free instead. Also fortunately, there was a stack of towels in the room — the masseurs had stolen their robes and their clothes!

Next they had to find a way out of the room. Spencer spotted an air vent and managed to climb into it, but after crawling along the duct for several minutes he emerged — through another vent on the far side of the same room!

They were almost ready to give up when the door to their room opened! A Japanese man in one of the massage parlor's robes stood there.

"Let's go!" Spencer told Mrs. Benson, and together they hurried out the door. They had to get back to the hotel and find the kids!

Carly had had enough. "Freddie, you're a boy," she told him, "get in there and break it up! Come on, get in there."

Freddie shook his head. "I don't wanna," he whined. But Carly pushed him toward the battling pair anyway.

"Go! Go!" she urged him.

Finally Freddie sighed — he never could say no to her. "'Kay, fine, I will." He walked over to Kyoko and Yuki. "Guys!" he called to them. "Guys, seriously! Just break it up! This isn't—" He stepped a little too close, though. Just as Kyoko's foot snapped up toward Yuki's head, Yuki ducked to one side, and the blow caught Freddie solidly in the face instead, knocking him to the ground.

"Freddie!" Carly ran over to him.

"Okay, that is definitely goin' on iCarly-dot-com," she heard Sam say behind her, but Carly was more concerned with Freddie. She helped him sit up and examined his face.

"Does my eye look okay?" he asked plaintively.

Carly grimaced. "Yes," she told him, but even she didn't believe herself. His eye was already turning black-and-blue. Man, for someone with her own Web show, she was a terrible actress sometimes!

Freddie knew her too well to be fooled. "For real?"

Fine, time for the truth. "No," Carly admitted. "It's all black-and—" she touched it tentatively but quickly pulled her hand away. "Eww, it's throbbing." She couldn't help backing away and shaking her hand as if trying to get something gross off it. "Eww, eww, eww!"

Sam walked over to them. As usual, she didn't even ask if Freddie was okay. Instead she sighed. "All right, this fight's gettin' old," she declared. She handed Freddie back his video camera and continued on past them to where Kyoko and Yuki were still trading blows. Sam timed her entrance carefully, then stepped between the pair and grabbed each one by an arm. The next thing anyone knew, the Japanese duo was on the ground.

"That's how we do it in Seattle," Sam told the stunned pair. She rejoined Carly and Freddie as Kyoko and Yuki picked themselves up again. Kyoko checked her arms and wrists, then nodded at Yuki. Did that mean they were done fighting?

"I'm really sorry Sam had to get physical with you guys," Carly told them.

"I'm sorry your foot had to get physical with my eye!" Freddie added, still keeping one hand pressed to his face.

Sam wasn't about to be left out. "I'm sorry I haven't eaten anything in four hours!" Carly glared at her, but Sam just pointed at her middle. "Well, listen to my stomach!"

Somehow Carly found her head pressed to her friend's midriff. "I don't want to listen to—" She recoiled. "Oh my God, it sounds like Chewbacca!" She could still hear Sam's stomach growling after she'd straightened up.

Kyoko's sigh interrupted them. "It is we who owe you an apology—" she explained sadly.

"—for ruining your trip to Japan—" Yuki cut in.

"—and any chance for either of our Web shows to win at the iWeb Awards," Kyoko finished. Carly couldn't help but stare. How did they finish each other's sentences like that?

"To apologize," Yuki continued, "please allow us to present you with a special gift."

"Why a gift?" Freddie wanted to know.

Kyoko smiled and bowed. "It's a Japanese tradition to give someone a gift after you cause them trouble," she explained.

"Oh, that's so nice!" Leave it to Sam to get greedy. "Where is it?"

Now Yuki bowed. "It is in our van." He and Kyoko turned toward the van.

"Yes. We will both go get your gift —" Kyoko offered.

"—while the three of you stand there," Yuki concluded. Really, it was uncanny. Carly was lucky to finish her own sentences, let alone anyone else's! She wondered if the pair wrote the same way. If she were to email Kyoko, would she only get half an email back?

But really, enough was enough. "You guys don't have to give us anything," she assured them.

Sam elbowed her in the side. "Don't disrespect their traditions," she hissed. "Is it expensive?" she wanted to know.

Kyoko and Yuki both nodded. "It is very special," Yuki promised.

"Just stay right there," Kyoko warned.

Yuki added, "And we'll be right back."

They backed up to the van and climbed in. Which made Carly wonder. The front seat wasn't that big, and she'd been staring at it for the past few hours. There hadn't been any presents there that she could see. Maybe it was in the glove compartment? But why would anyone carry a gift just in case they upset someone else? That didn't make a whole lot of sense!

Her musings were interrupted as she heard the unmistakable sound of a car engine. At first she thought it was another vehicle coming down the road, but then she realized the sound was coming from Yuki's van!

"Hey, I thought the van ran outta gas," Carly said aloud. Just then the van took off with a squeal of tires and sped off down the road. In seconds it was gone.

The three of them stood there, watching it go.

"I don't think we're getting a gift," Freddie commented after a minute.

Sam remained hopeful. "Maybe they're driving somewhere to get it," she suggested.

But now it all added up. "No," Carly cried out, suddenly furious at the comedy duo and at herself for not putting it all together before. "They did all this on purpose so they could ditch us and then go win the iWeb Award!"

Sam shook her head. "So they're definitely not giving us a present?" she asked finally.

Carly's *"Nooo!"* was barely more than a howl. How could she have been so stupid? Kyoko and Yuki had never been lost! The whole thing had been planned from the start! She mentally kicked herself — no wonder they'd been able to finish each other's sentences! They'd probably rehearsed the whole thing beforehand! And now here they were, stuck out in the middle of nowhere — again! — with no car and no cell phone and no way to make it to the iWeb Awards on time!

Could this trip get any worse?

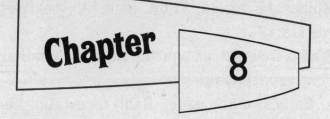
Apparently, it could.

"I feel like we've been walking for nine years," Sam complained. They were trudging along the empty road — it had seemed like a better option than standing still or, as Carly had briefly considered, sitting down and crying. And at least they had a direction — they were going the same way Kyoko and Yuki had gone. Carly assumed the scheming Japanese duo had made a beeline for the iWeb Awards after ditching them.

"I can't believe I got a black eye," Freddie whined. He probed gently around it with his fingers. "Ah, it's still throbbing!"

"Yeah, yeah," Sam snapped at him, "so's my head from all your yappin'!" Carly considered pointing out that Sam had been doing most of the complaining so far, but decided she couldn't be bothered.

Instead she asked, "How long till the iWeb Awards start?"

Freddie checked his watch. "Less than half an hour," he reported glumly.

On Carly's other side, Sam threw up her hands. "There's no way we're gonna make it," she announced. "Not possible, zero chance."

"Hey, that's the spirit," Carly told her dryly.

"I'm just being realistic," her best friend argued.

Carly tried to stay upbeat. "Look, I'm sure Spencer and Freddie's mom are doing everything they can to find us." She stopped walking for a second. Her feet were killing her! "And anyway," she continued, "aren't you the one who gave us the 'only losers give up' speech?"

Sam shrugged. "I dunno. I don't listen to the things I say."

"Well, you did," Carly reminded her, "and you were right, so let's not give up now."

Freddie scuffed his shoe on the asphalt. "Well, what are we supposed to do?" he asked.

"I dunno," Carly admitted, "but it's not help-ing for you guys to keep talking about how

82

hungry and miserable you are." She focused on Freddie. "We all know that your eye is black and throbbing"—then looked over at Sam—"and we all know you're starving, so let's forget that stuff and try to think positively, all right?" Carly remembered her Melanie Higgles character and tried to channel that inner cheerleader. "Maybe Spencer and Freddie's mom will find us in time, and maybe they'll bring eye ointment and cheeseburgers." She had to raise her voice over a dull rumbling nearby. "I just think if we all try to keep a positive attitude, then maybe we'll—"

The rumbling increased to a heavy rattle as a truck roared by. Its rear tire hit a puddle in the road just as it drove past them, splashing filthy, muddy water on all three of them.

Carly just stood there, her mouth open. She was dripping wet, she was cold and slimy, and she was covered head to toe in gross yellowish mud.

"Okay, that did it," she admitted sadly. "Now I'm depressed."

Sam and Freddie nodded. There wasn't anything else to say to that. So they turned as one and started walking again. Carly figured at this rate they might reach the hotel — and be dry — by the time they needed to head home.

Meanwhile, Spencer and Mrs. Benson had finally reached the hotel themselves. Everyone stared as they'd crossed the lobby wearing nothing but towels, but they didn't stop. Instead they raced up to their rooms, got the maid to let them in, and put on proper clothes again. Then they ran back down to the lobby.

Spencer rushed up to the front desk. A man was talking to the hotel clerk already, but Spencer pushed past him. He noticed that the man was holding a pink poodle hand puppet. The man and the puppet had on matching tuxedos. *The Japanese are so strange*, Spencer thought.

"Excuse me," he told the desk clerk. "We have an emergency."

"*Excusez-moi*," the man with the puppet cut in. He sure didn't sound Japanese! "I am in the middle —"

"I don't have time to talk to you," Spencer said, cutting the other man off.

That got the stranger in a huff. Both he and his hand puppet started shouting at Spencer in what sounded like French or maybe Chinese. All Spencer knew for certain was that it was distracting him from trying to find Carly.

"Why am I arguing with a poodle with a mustache?" he asked no one in particular. Then he yanked the puppet off the man's hand. There was a little Japanese boy right behind them, and Spencer turned, presenting the boy with the puppet. "Here," he told the boy. "He's yours if you run away."

The boy gave him a big smile and took off, clutching the puppet tightly.

"Oompé!" the man in the tux shouted. It sounded like a curse word. "Oompé, come back! Oompé!" He took off after the boy.

That meant Spencer could focus on the hotel clerk again. "Listen," he said quickly, "my little sister and her two friends were kidnapped by evil Japanese Web comedians and we don't know where they are, so if you could please call the —"

Just then Mrs. Benson shouted, "Oh my God!"

Spencer yelped, startled, and turned to stare at her. "What?!"

"The chip!" she told him. "In all this confusion, I completely forgot about the chip."

"Chip? What chip?" Spencer and the hotel clerk both asked.

Mrs. Benson was busy digging through her purse. "As soon as Freddie was old enough to toddle," she explained, "I had a locator chip put in his head by a questionable doctor in Venezuela."

Spencer and the hotel clerk looked at each other. The clerk looked as confused as Spencer felt. "You chipped Freddie?!" Spencer asked.

Mrs. Benson nodded, still digging. "Oh, I chipped him because I love him."

The hotel clerk held up a large bag of potato chips, but Spencer shook his head. He thought he'd got it. "You mean a locator chip like a GPS kinda thing?"

Mrs. Benson nodded and paused her search to glare at him. "Yes! But you can never tell him —"

"I won't, I won't," he reassured her. "Just — how do we find him?!"

She smiled and pulled a cool-looking handheld GPS unit from her purse. "With this!"

She switched it on, and at once a computerized

female voice emerged. "Welcome to Global Net," it said. "Please stand by while we locate Benson, Fredward."

Spencer stared at the GPS unit. He loved gadgets of all sorts, and GPS units were some of the coolest things around! "That is insane!" he muttered. His fingers itched to play with the GPS. Mrs. Benson had a death grip on it, though, and she shushed him as she stared at the screen, waiting impatiently. After a few seconds a light started to blink, and both of them got excited. Then it spoke again.

"Benson, Fredward: located," the GPS reported. "Twelve point-seven miles northeast."

"Got him!" Mrs. Benson crowed. She took off for the hotel's front door at a run. "Don't worry, Freddie!" she shouted, "Momma's comin'!"

"Spencer's also coming!" Spencer shouted as he raced to catch up with her. He just hoped Carly and the others were okay.

They'd been walking for a while when Freddie stopped and frowned, rubbing the back of his head. "You guys hear that?" he asked.

Carly shook her head. So did Sam. "Hear what?"

Freddie felt the back of his head again. Then he glared at them and at the dark, empty night all around. "All right, what's going on?" he demanded.

"What do you mean?" Carly looked at Sam, who shrugged.

"I dunno," Freddie told her. "It's like I can just barely hear this faint beeping, like in the back of my head." He patted his head some more. "It's so weird."

Sam snorted. "*You're* so weird," she corrected.

"We're all weird," Carly pointed out. "Let's keep walking."

They started moving again, but every so often Freddie felt the back of his head and stared around them. Carly had no idea what he expected to see. Probably his mom leaping out of the bushes to save them. Right now, that sounded fine to Carly, too.

"I still don't see why we have to carry Sam," Freddie commented later. He and Carly were lugging Sam stretched out between them.

Carly started to answer, then realized she didn't know either. "Yeah," she agreed, looking down at Sam. "Why are we carrying you?" She wasn't even entirely sure how that had happened — all she could remember was that one minute they'd all been walking side by side and the next she and Freddie were carrying Sam.

"We're taking turns," Sam explained easily, as if it were the most obvious thing in the world. "If we ever get lost in Japan again, I'm gonna carry you guys."

Carly rolled her eyes. "Uh-huh." Because they were *so* planning on making a habit out of this! Freddie muttered something similar.

Yet they continued to carry her. At least for a little while.

They'd set Sam on her own two feet a while ago, and they'd been walking long enough that the mud had all dried and was starting to crack when Carly heard something approaching them. It was a deep buzzing noise that kind of sounded like a really big bee. Maybe a lawnmower? Or — ?

Sam and Freddie heard it, too, and all three of

them squinted up ahead, just as a pair of blinding lights pierced the night. A car!

Then Carly was sure she must be dreaming, because she heard a voice shouting. In English. A voice she knew.

"Hey!" it said. "You guys! Carly!"

"Spencer?" Carly shaded her face and tried to see past the spots in front of her eyes. "Spencer?"

The car — which turned out to be a tiny little Japanese taxicab — screeched to a halt right beside them. As it shut off its headlights Carly was finally able to see properly again. Someone burst from the passenger side before the car had even rolled to a complete stop and raced toward them. It was Freddie's mom!

"Mrs. Benson!" Carly shouted. She was actually glad to see her!

Then a tall, gangly figure tumbled out of the top of the car. Carly couldn't help the tears of relief that burst from her eyes. Only one person in the entire world fell over like that. She was already running to his side as he sat up and started to push himself off the ground.

"Spencer!" she shouted. Then she was hugging her brother, who was hugging her back.

"I'm okay, I'm okay!" he assured her, hugging her tight. "Don't worry about me!" He reached out and swept Sam up into a big hug as well.

Sam put up with that for all of three seconds, which showed just how happy she was to see them. Then she pulled out of his grip. "Hey!" she demanded. "Did anyone bring any food?"

Mrs. Benson was busy trying to wipe all the mud off Freddie — with baby wipes. He was trying to get her to stop, but Carly could tell he was secretly glad for the attention.

Carly was still trying to get over her shock at their sudden appearance. "How'd you find us?" she asked Spencer.

He grinned. "Oh, Mrs. Benson had a chip" — out of the corner of her eye Carly saw Mrs. Benson making frantic motions at him — "chip . . . chipew . . . Chippewa! She had a Chippewa Indian show us the way." Carly stared at him and he shrugged helplessly. Clearly there was a story here, but she had a feeling she wasn't going to get

91

the truth out of him — at least, not while Freddie's mom was within earshot.

Mrs. Benson was suddenly distracted, however — she had finally removed enough of the mud on Freddie's face to notice the black eye. He assured her he was fine, but that didn't stop her from wringing her hands.

Surprisingly, it was Sam who saved Freddie from further embarrassment. "The iWeb Awards!" she shouted.

Carly took the cue. "Freddie, how long till the iWeb Awards start?" she asked.

He glanced at his watch. "Ah, um, ah," he stalled. He sighed. "About five minutes." Then he brightened again. "But the comedy shows go last!"

Sam got a determined look on her face, the one that usually meant she was about to do something stupid. "Well, c'mon," she urged the rest of them. "Let's try and make it!"

They all scrambled for the cab. It was too small for them all to fit easily, though. Fortunately there was a sunroof, and Spencer crawled in back and then stood up through it while Sam, Carly, and Freddie squeezed in around him. But he kept having to pull his legs up higher and higher, until he was actually sitting on top of the cab's roof!

"Okay, everyone in?" Carly asked after Mrs. Benson had pulled the door shut.

"Not really!" Spencer shouted down. But the cab driver revved up and took off anyway. He didn't get far — Spencer tumbled right off the roof and down the back of the car, landing on the road behind them with a thud.

"Stop! Stop!" Carly shouted, pounding on the driver's seat with her fist. He obligingly screeched to a halt, then backed up. There was another thud, and Spencer disappeared from the view out the rear window. Alarmed, Carly managed to twist past Freddie and his mom and out of the car. She was surprised to find her brother stretched out on the ground just below the car's rear bumper.

"Spencer! Spencer!" He glanced up at her. She didn't see any injuries. "Why are you on the ground?" she asked him.

"Oh, just bein' lazy," he told her. She was pretty sure that wasn't true, but there wasn't time to argue. She dragged him back toward the car and pushed him in ahead of her, and he wriggled his

93

way back out the sunroof again. This time, though, he kept his feet firmly planted inside.

"Go, go, go," he shouted down at the driver once he was situated. "We're gonna be late!"

The driver muttered something in Japanese — Carly thought she recognized some of the same words Kyoko and Yuki had used while pretending to argue — and took off again. They were finally on their way to the iWeb Awards!

Carly looked up and laughed — Spencer was standing up through the tiny cab's equally tiny sunroof, his entire upper body out of the car, and he was clearly loving it. He had a big grin on his face, his mouth wide open, and his tongue sticking out — he looked like a big shaggy dog. Then she looked again.

"Spencer?" He couldn't hear her over the wind — the cab was going really fast! "Spencer!" That got his attention. "Why are your teeth green?"

Her brother started to say something, shook his head, then tried again. "It's a long story," he finally shouted back.

In the front seat, Mrs. Benson turned around. "That massage was nothing but a set-up," she explained. "The cousins of those crazy so-called friends of yours treated us to a seaweed wrap, all right! They trussed us up like two Thanksgiving turkeys! Then they stole our clothes, locked us in, and left!"

Carly, Sam, and Freddie gasped.

"How did you get out?" Carly asked.

"Spencer chewed through the seaweed," Mrs. Benson told her.

"Only mine," Spencer quickly corrected. "I used a sword on hers." Freddie clearly wasn't sure whether to be relieved or horrified by this revelation.

"Then we banged on the door until another customer let us out, and ran back to the hotel to get more clothes and go look for you," Mrs. Benson finished.

"Well, it could have been a long story," Spencer muttered from up above.

"I'm just glad you're both okay," Carly told them. She patted Spencer's knee.

"Yeah, it would've been a real shame if anything happened to you," Sam said. Then she brightened. "Hey, do you still have any of that seaweed?"

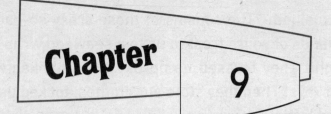

Chapter 9

"**H**i! Hello? Excuse us!"

Carly and the others raced up the iWeb Awards studio driveway. The cab was already disappearing behind them — the driver had barely waited to be paid — and they had wasted no time heading for the security guard on duty. They had to get inside, and quickly! Carly could see the show's opening graphics, displayed on a little monitor set into the wall right beside the security door. It looked the show was only just starting. They'd made it!

They all started talking at once, explaining who they were and why they were late. But they stopped when the guard held up a little sign. It said I DO NOT SPEAK SPANISH.

What?

"I wasn't speaking Spanish," Carly told him.

In response, he flipped a new page over the same sign. Now it read I DO NOT SPEAK ENGLISH.

"C'mon," Sam growled, "let's just go in." They pushed forward, but the guard blocked their path. He pointed at a sign behind them. It read PERFORMERS ONLY and then had several lines in other languages, probably all saying the same thing. The guard then told them something in Japanese.

"We are performers!" Carly informed him. She was getting upset — they hadn't come all this way just to be stopped by some silly security guard and his hand signs!

But the guard refused to budge. They kept talking at him, and he flipped the sign again. Now it read HAPPY BIRTHDAY.

"It's nobody's birthday!" Carly all but screamed at him. "You're so random!"

She glanced over at the monitor again. The host, a skinny guy in a short-sleeved black button-down shirt and a thin red tie, was saying, ". . . to kick off the iWeb Awards, we have a little somethin' special for ya. Are ya ready?!" The crowd roared its approval.

"Don't you have tickets or passes or something?" Mrs. Benson was asking Freddie.

"Yeah, of course," Freddie told her. "They were in our suitcase that Freight Dog dropped into the lake."

Spencer shouldered past them. "Here, lemme talk to the guy." He turned to the guard and said something in Japanese. The guard looked surprised, then he slapped Spencer across the face. Hard. "Okay, maybe I didn't say that quite right," Spencer acknowledged, rubbing his cheek. "*Ow*!"

Now the guard started shouting at them, gesturing all the while. Carly couldn't really blame him. Here were these strange Americans, all covered in mud, who didn't speak a word of Japanese, and they expected to be let in during the iWeb Awards with no IDs or tickets or anything. She probably wouldn't let them in either!

But that didn't change the fact that they were supposed to be here, and they had to get inside. Carly pointed at the monitor. "We're missing the show," she pointed out. "We need to go inside!"

The security guard held up a different sign.

98

This one didn't even have any words — it was just a cartoon of a cute little bunny rabbit.

"Okay," Sam announced. She was clearly fed up. "When I say 'now,' everybody scream and run inside — he can't stop us all." Mrs. Benson started to protest, but Sam spoke over her. "Now!" Then she screamed and ran for the door. The others followed.

But the security guard was ready for them. He raised a whistle to his lips and blew a shrill blast on it even as he stepped forward to keep them from reaching the door. Seconds later, four more guards appeared and rushed in front of Sam and the others. Sam kicked the first guard in the ankle, then leaped on his back and started to give him a vicious noogie, which made him scream. Two other guards pulled her off. Everyone was yelling, and the first guard kept waving his sign, each time with a different picture or saying.

Carly couldn't take it any more. "All right!" she screamed. Her voice cut through the din, and everyone stopped dead and stared at her. "Just forget it." She turned and walked away, but couldn't help stopping and pointing at the largest, heaviest guard, who was wearing a really obvious hairpiece. "That is fake hair!" she announced to the world. For some reason, declaring that made her feel better.

Sam, Freddie, and Mrs. Benson followed her. Spencer stayed behind long enough to shout something at the guards in Japanese — Carly had no idea what he'd said, but the guards all burst out laughing as a result. Judging from her brother's expression as he joined them, she didn't think that was the response he'd been hoping for.

Carly stopped a little ways down the driveway. She could still hear the monitor behind her. The Japanese announcer was just saying, "Next up are the nominees for Best Cooking Show!"

"I can't believe they won't let us in!" Carly moaned. To come all this way and then be stopped just outside the door — it was worse than if they'd never come at all!

Freddie was clearly thinking the same thing. "We came this close and now we finally got here and we're still gonna lose by default," he groused.

"So now what?" Sam demanded. But Carly just shook her head. She was out of ideas.

Mrs. Benson studied them. "Why don't we all go back to our hotel and pack up?" she suggested gently.

But for once, Freddie stood up to his mom. "No!" he told her sharply. "Do you not get that *iCarly* is really important to me" — he gestured toward Carly and Sam — "and to them? This was a big deal for us." Mrs. Benson just stared at him — it was one of the only times Carly had ever seen Freddie talk back to her.

Sam sighed. "Whatever, let's just get outta here."

But Mrs. Benson surprised them all by saying, "No." She squared her shoulders. "I'm going back over to those security guards," she announced.

"But they don't speak English—" Carly reminded her.

Mrs. Benson smiled. "I'm going to distract them. When I do, you all run inside that door." She approached the guards and smiled at them as everyone watched. Then she reached up and snatched the big guard's toupee and ran away, screaming and waving the hairpiece over her head. Immediately the guards chased after her.

Carly exchanged shocked glances with the others for a second. None of them could believe that Freddie's mom, who was always so cautious and so uptight, had just done that! It was one of the most amazing and selfless acts Carly had ever seen.

Spencer was the first to snap out of it. "Now!" he reminded the others. "C'mon! Let's go!" He pushed them toward the empty guard station and the now-unguarded stage door. "Go, go, go!"

Carly, Sam, and Freddie didn't need any more urging. They ran for the door, pulled it open, and raced inside.

Once the door slammed shut behind them, Carly motioned for everyone to stop and find a place to hide. That was easy enough — they were backstage in what had to be a prep area for the show, and there were large scenery pieces all over the place. There were also all sorts of people walking around — some of them had to be performers, judging from their clothes, but others looked more like stagehands, tech crew, and various other staff. When there was a gap in the traffic, Carly led the others in a mad dash across the floor to a piece of scenery some fifteen feet away. More people came through, and they all ducked out of sight until the footsteps and voices had faded away.

"See anyone?" Spencer whispered after a second of silence.

Freddie peeked out around a corner. "All clear," he reported.

Sam nodded. "Let's go!" She burst from behind their cover, the others right behind her, and ran for the sign that said STAGE — only to run right into a group of men. Men in uniforms. Really familiar-looking uniforms. And really familiar-looking — and angry — men.

The security guards had found them!

This time they weren't alone. There was another man with them, a short stout man a bit older than the others and in a nicer uniform — slacks and a suit jacket with a white button-down shirt and a tie. Carly guessed he was the security chief.

"Hi," she said, glancing around desperately for a way out. She noticed the big guard in the back. "I see you found your hair." Before she could try anything else, the guards dashed forward and grabbed their arms, holding them fast.

The security chief snarled something in Japanese, and the guards quickly hauled them away. As they were led deeper into the building — at least they weren't being tossed out just yet — they passed another monitor. Carly glanced at it and groaned to see a beret-wearing man and his pink poodle hand puppet. It was Henri P'Twa and Oompé! They were sitting on a bench, wearing matching tuxedos. And the sign behind them read NOMINEE FOR BEST COMEDY WEB SHOW. Time was running out!

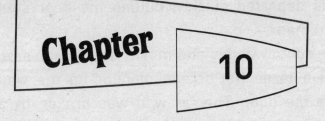

Chapter 10

"Ow, take it easy!" Carly complained. The guards had dragged her and her friends down several hallways to a blank wooden door, which they had pushed open. Then they roughly shoved everyone inside the room.

"Freddie!"

Everyone glanced up. There were already two people in the room — Mrs. Benson and the strange guard with the little signs! He had her by the arm, but now she pulled free to sweep Freddie into one of her big "mama bear" hugs.

Carly took stock of their new accommodations as the security chief and the big guard followed them in. The chief said something sharp to the others, no doubt giving them orders and possibly chewing them out for being schooled by a trio of kids and their guardians, and the other guards departed quickly, pulling the door shut behind them.

The room was big and mostly empty, she saw. It had a large flat-screen monitor on the wall beside the door. The far wall was broken by a wide window that peered into the neighboring room. Below those were a variety of cords and jacks, making the place look like a larger version of Freddie's production setup in their loft. One of the side walls was covered by a row of industrial shelves holding enormous spools of cable and what looked like audio-visual equipment. Through the window she could see what was obviously a control booth, filled with people and monitors and yet more cables and switches. Henri P'Twa was still performing, she noticed. The monitor in here didn't have the sound on, and she was fine with that — having to listen to that man and his puppet twice already had been more than enough.

The security chief was glaring at them, she suddenly realized. And now he was speaking — but of course they didn't understand a word of it.

"None of us speak Japanese," Spencer told him. Carly was glad to see her brother was refraining

106

from flexing his language skills again. The last time he'd spoken to the guards they'd laughed at him — the time before that, one had slapped him. If he tried again he'd probably land them all in prison!

The guards were conferring, and finally the one with the signs handed the chief a thick, worn-looking paperback.

"Oh good," Carly told the others when she finally made sense of its title. "He's got a Japanese-English Dictionary." She couldn't help the twinge of hope that flared up inside. They were already in the building! The iWeb Awards stage couldn't be far away! And they weren't actually late for their appearance yet — they could still make it!

She watched anxiously as the security chief flipped through the pages. So did the others. "Okay, he's lookin' up something," Sam commented.

"This is progress," Spencer agreed.

The chief stopped flipping. Then he held the book up and showed the page he'd found to his two subordinates. Both of them stared at it a second before grunting and nodding. At least they liked it!

Then the security chief cleared his throat. "*Shhh*, he's gonna say something," Freddie warned. The others hushed him quickly.

The chief consulted the book again and cleared his throat a second time. Then he slowly, carefully said, "Heh-looo."

Carly sighed. So did the others. They all looked at each other.

"Hello," they all replied together. So much for that glimmer of hope!

Carly saw motion on the screen and almost wailed when she realized it was Henri P'Twa bowing. Oompé and a second puppet, a cat on Henri's other hand, bowed as well.

Then the host came on. Carly still couldn't make out any words, but she could guess what he was saying, especially since she was pretty sure she saw his lips form "*iCarly*" — he was telling the audience that they hadn't shown up for the awards. Which meant he'd be moving on to the third — now second — contestant for Best Comedy Web Show: *Kyoko and Yuki*!

Sure enough, the screen behind the stage

flashed the title graphics from Kyoko and Yuki's show.

Freddie had noticed as well, and Sam did just as Kyoko and Yuki appeared on stage. They were wearing matching tan pants and a red-and-white-striped polo shirt—a single shirt. The shirt had been designed so each of them had his or her own collar, and their outer arms were visible, but the inner arms were concealed. They looked like the preppy version of a two-headed monster!

"Aw, great," Sam fumed. "We were supposed to go on before them."

Mrs. Benson stepped toward the security guards. "Those," she stated, gesturing toward the screen, "are the Internet delinquents who tricked these children! And us!" But the guards clearly didn't understand her—and just as clearly didn't care.

"We were seaweeded to massage tables!" Spencer added, also to no effect.

At least the chief was still thumbing through the dictionary. But Carly couldn't hold back her groan when he finally raised his head and tried out his newest word:

"Lasagna."

On the screen, Kyoko and Yuki were sitting at a simple kitchen table, playing the two-headed diner to the hilt. Yuki was trying to eat soup from a large cup but Kyoko had acquired a trumpet from somewhere — now she blasted Yuki right in the ears, and surprised him so much that he spit out soup everywhere. Carly was sure it was very funny, but right now she really didn't feel like laughing.

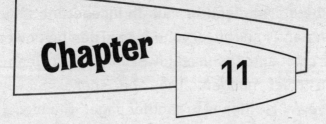

Chapter 11

"Look," Sam was shouting at the security guards, "Kyoko and Yuki cheated!" She was livid, though Carly knew some of that was simply from hunger. Hunger made her best friend crazy. Unfortunately, Sam was always hungry.

Freddie was right beside her, their occasional bickering forgotten in this common cause. "That's how I got this black eye!" he explained, pointing at his shiner.

"These kids are nominees!" Mrs. Benson was trying to explain in her loudest voice.

And of course Spencer had to have his say—about something. "Why does your soap look like candy?" he asked.

The security chief was ignoring all of them and focusing on his translation book. Finally he seemed to find what he was looking for. He nodded to his men, and the big guard stepped forward, raised his arms, and let out an incoherent shout that instantly shut everyone else. Then he bowed to the chief and gestured toward the *iCarly* team.

The chief nodded. Then he spoke. Slowly. "I. Have. A." He flipped to another page. "Bladder... infection."

Carly just stared at him, and he nodded fervently. Okay, so he had a bladder infection! Poor guy! So what?

"Can't you guys go get someone that speaks English?" Spencer pleaded. That provoked a response from the chief, but of course it was in Japanese, so they had no idea what he was saying. Probably "Sorry, I don't speak English — can't you say it in Japanese?"

"Forget it," Sam snarled, turning her back on the guards. "These donut holes can't understand anything."

Carly slumped. She watched the guards, wishing she could think of some way to communicate with them. Anything! English obviously wasn't working, but then neither was Japanese — at least, not Spencer's version of it. So where did that leave them? Besides stuck in a utility room while Kyoko and Yuki ran away with their prize?

She glanced over at the monitor again, and wished she hadn't. Yuki had given up on the soup, but Kyoko still had her trumpet firmly in hand, and she blared it at him again — he jerked back, and would have fallen off his chair if they hadn't been attached. The guard with the signs had glanced over there as well, and he was laughing. Even without sound Kyoko and Yuki's actions were funny.

Then it hit Carly. Without sound, they were still funny! That was it!

She turned to Sam and grabbed her by the shoulders. "We have to communicate with these guys," she insisted.

"We can't," her best friend replied.

"We can't with words," Carly agreed. That got a "huh?" out of Sam, but Carly forged on ahead. "Let's act it out for 'em," she suggested.

"Act what out?"

"Everything that's happened to us since we got to Japan," Carly replied. Maybe then they'd understand what was going on!

Freddie had been listening, of course, and he nodded. "Do it!" he agreed.

Sam nodded, convinced to at least give it a try. After all, what did they have to lose at this point?

"Okay!" Carly headed straight to the security chief, Sam right beside her. "You wanna know what happened?" They didn't understand her words, of course, but she suspected they got the tone. They certainly knew it was a question, because all three of them started nodding.

"Here's what happened," Sam offered. She glanced at Carly, urging her to get them started.

Carly took a deep breath. *Right, here it goes,* she thought. "We" — she gestured to Sam and herself — "do a comedy show on the Web," she explained. She moved her fingers as if she were typing on a keyboard.

"Y'know, a show" Sam looked around, saw a laptop lying on a crate nearby, and grabbed it, "on the Internet." She held it up facing the chief and gestured at the screen.

He had his arms crossed, but he nodded at the screen. Okay, he seemed to get "Internet," and possibly "show" as well. But how to convey "comedy"?

"Comedy," Carly repeated slowly. "Like—" She started laughing, great big laughs while holding her sides. Sam joined in. They pointed at each other, made silly faces, and laughed even louder. Then they stopped completely.

The chief was still looking stony-faced. Okay, time for Plan B.

Carly raced past him—right toward the guard with the sign. Sam, realizing at once what she was doing, headed for the big guard. Then they started tickling the two men, who convulsed with laughter. "See?" she asked the chief over her shoulder. "Comedy!"

Beside them, on the monitor, Kyoko and Yuki were still sitting at the table, but now they were eating an ear of corn. A three-foot-long ear of corn! At the same time! They were each holding an end, and both taking bites, but Carly could tell even with the sound off that they were arguing about it. The fact that their rivals were clearly entertaining the crowd only motivated her more.

"We got an invitation," she continued. She mimed opening a mailbox, finding an envelope, and opening it. Sam "read" it over her shoulder and pointed to where it said something, and then they both started screaming and fist-bumping and high-fiving. "To come here!" Carly added. She pointed to the ground. Sam pointed to the monitor. "Here, to the iWeb Awards!"

"iWeb Awards," the chief confirmed. At least those words he understood!

"Yes, exactly!" Carly agreed. "But we live a long way away." She put one hand to her eyes, as if scanning the horizon. "Much too far to walk." She walked a few steps, then slumped and shook her head to show that wouldn't work.

"We had to get here fast," Sam added. She slid one hand across the other fast, like a rocket taking off. The chief mimicked her. "Yes, fast!"

"So we drove to the airport," Carly explained, gesturing like she was driving a car and honking the horn at imaginary rude people in their way, "and then all five of us" — she indicated Spencer, who was standing in the corner leaning on the shelves, Mrs. Benson who was sitting on an equipment crate beside him, and Freddie who was leaning against the wall of the control booth — "got on a horrible airplane."

"Airplane," Sam repeated. She held her arms out straight and zoomed toward the guards, making engine noises. Carly joined her. The guards seemed taken aback, but they were nodding, too. Everyone knew what an airplane was! Carly felt a thrill, the same one she got when performing on *iCarly*. It was working!

While she was running in circles around the security chief, Carly noticed that Freddie was the only one not paying attention to them. Instead he was studying the row of cables and jacks right beside him — the ones that led into the control booth on the other side of that wall. She wondered what he was up to, but didn't have time to worry about it. Because now came the tricky part.

She came to a stop in front of the chief. "And the plane" — she held out her arms again — "was filled" — she raised her arms as if they were full — "with possi," she told him. She raised

117

her hands and made little chittering sounds. Did possi even make noise, she wondered? It had been too loud in the plane to tell. Well, whatever.

Sam shook her head. Even now she refused to accept that Freddie might be right about that term. "Many *possums*," she insisted. She grabbed Carly's hands and gestured with them.

The chief looked dumbfounded. And who could blame him? "Poo-sum?" he asked.

"Possum!" Carly snapped. Then she reminded herself that she had to stay focused — losing her temper would only anger the guards further. Sam had raced around to the chief's other side, and now both of them started making little rodent paws and faces at him and chittering like the world's largest, angriest mice. Or rats. Or possums. Possi? Whatever.

Behind her, Carly caught another glimpse of Freddie. He'd pulled out his video camera and was filming them. Well, why not, she decided. They could always show bits of it back home — assuming they ever got home again. She wondered if Japanese prisons had their own Web shows.

"So Freight Dog said we had to jump *out* of the plane!" she told the chief next. She gestured like airplane wings again, and then mimed diving.

"Jump!" Sam repeated, jumping up in the air.

"Joomp?" the chief asked. He was trying to understand them, at least—he was listening very seriously, and repeating words whenever he could. Not always right, but he definitely got points for effort.

"Jump!" Carly confirmed. She jumped again, as did Sam. Then the security chief started hopping up and down as well!

"Jump!" he shouted, smiling. He gestured to the guards behind him, and they took that as an order. They began jumping too.

"Yes!" Sam shouted in midair.

Carly continued jumping. "We had to jump," she repeated, "out of the plane!" She mimed a plane again.

"Jump!" the chief said again. He seemed to be enjoying this part.

Carly couldn't help noticing that, on the monitor, Kyoko and Yuki had left their table. They were standing in front of it now, bowing to the audience.

That meant they were almost finished! She started to despair, but refused to give up — especially now that they were finally getting through to the guards!

There was something weird about the image on the monitor, though. It took her a second to realize why. The graphic that had been showing behind the comedy duo flickered a bit. Then it disappeared completely, leaving a black screen behind them. Was that supposed to happen?

Now it was flickering again. But the chief still hadn't gotten the whole "out of a plane" thing — he seemed stuck on "jump," which he kept repeating — so Carly turned her attention back to that. Sam had climbed up on one of the equipment crates, and Carly joined her. They held hands, then screamed and jumped off, racing toward the guards, who backed away quickly. Carly and Sam started jumping up and down in front of them, screaming and waving their hands, and the guards cowered and screamed and flailed right back. They were right in front of the door, too! If only they would move out of the way! But Carly knew running wasn't an option anymore.

They had to show them what was going on. They just had to!

"We all jumped," she continued, turning back to the chief again and indicating Spencer, Mrs. Benson, and Freddie, who she noticed was crouched down by the wall and still filming them. "But Spencer with his parachute" — she swung her arms wide over her head and swayed like she had when they'd floated to the ground.

"Parachute?" the chief asked. He nodded quickly. Was "parachute" the same in Japanese as in English, Carly wondered? If so, cool — she knew a Japanese word!

"With his parachute," she started again, motioning Mrs. Benson to step into the middle of the room. "His feet hit Freddie's mom in the head, and knocked her down."

Sam had found a broom leaning against one of the shelves, and now she hoisted it high. "Kinda like this!"

Hearing her, Mrs. Benson half-turned. "Wait," she asked quickly, "you're not gonna —" but whatever else she meant to ask got caught off as Sam whacked her in the back of the head with the broom, knocking Mrs. Benson to the floor.

Carly couldn't help laughing. Especially since, for once, Freddie was making no move to help his mom up.

"But a nice police officer," Carly said with a salute, "found us and gave us a ride into Tokyo." She did the "driving a car" gesture again.

"Tokyo!" the chief agreed. He gestured around them.

"Yes, here!" Carly agreed. "To the Hotel Nakamura!"

"Ah, Nakamura." That got a nod from the chief. Of course he'd know the name of the hotel! And all the show's nominees were staying there! Was he starting to get it? Carly hoped so—she knew they were almost out of time. She was afraid to glance at the monitor again, for fear that she'd see the award show's closing credits—or, worse, Kyoko and Yuki accepting their award! Instead she kept her eyes resolutely on the chief and on Sam, who was now explaining what had happened next.

"And when we were checkin' into our hotel," Sam was saying, gesturing as if signing a register and then drawing a big building with her hands, "this French guy—" she stuck up her nose and snorted.

"Who's also a nominee," Carly hastened to add.

"—kept buttin' in with his stupid puppet," Sam stepped in front of her and finished. She held up her hand and made little puppet motions with it.

That one was clearly beyond the chief. "Poopit?" he asked. He raised the dictionary a little, as if about to consult it, and Carly knew she had to prevent that at all costs—if he got into that book again they'd still be trading the names of Italian menu items and medical issues hours from now!

"And he was all," she put on a deliberately horrible French accent, raising her right hand to show the puppet, "'This is my poopit.'"

Sam flanked the chief again. "'Look at my beautiful poopit,'" she insisted, shoving her hand in his face.

She and Carly were getting into it now. "'I need a separate room for my poopit,'" Carly demanded. She and Sam both started chanting about the "sweet poopit," waving their arms and dancing around.

"Poopit?" the chief repeated several times. So did the two guards. Carly thought they understood. But even if they didn't, at least they were laughing.

"Then Kyoko and Yuki showed up at our door," Carly continued. She mimed knocking on a door, opening it, and smiling pleasantly. Now she wished she'd never been so nice to them!

"Kyoko and Yuki?" The chief definitely knew those names!

"Yes, Kyoko and Yuki!" Sam spat on the ground, which made the chief scratch his head. "I mean, Kyoko and Yuki!" She smiled and then made Kyoko's "crying face."

"They offered to take us shopping," Carly told him, taking his arm and leading him around the room, picking out imaginary clothes and holding them up against him or setting imaginary hats on his friend. "So we got in their car" — the

124

driving motion again, which the chief imitated, nodding — "and drove a long, long way!" She scanned the horizon again, and glanced at an imaginary watch, shaking her head.

"They started arguing," Sam picked up. She and Carly began sniping at each other, saying nonsense but letting their expressions and angry gestures get the point across. Actually, it was a lot like the end of their Melanie Higgles routine, except without the padded clubs. Or any clubs — she couldn't trust Sam not to actually beat on her!

"And we thought Kyoko and Yuki were fighting for real," Sam continued. She snapped a kick that just missed the chief's face.

Carly was bouncing up and down by now — they were nearing the end! "So, Sam broke up the fight by flipping them." She turned to her friend. "Sam?"

Sam was happy to oblige. She stepped over to where the two guards were still huddled in the corner, and quickly flipped the first one and then the other onto their backs. *Ouch!* That had to hurt on the hard cement floor! But Carly shrugged — it was their own fault! And even the chief was laughing! He said something in Japanese, pointed at Sam, and raised his arms like a champion. Sam nodded and raised her arms right back. Yes!

"Oh, tell them what happened to us," Spencer requested from his corner. Carly nodded and moved over to Sam's side again.

"And while we were with Kyoko and Yuki," she told the chief, gesturing toward Spencer, "my brother—"

"—and this lady," Sam added, pointing to Mrs. Benson. Both she and Spencer waved.

"They couldn't help us because they were getting massages from Kyoko and Yuki's cousins." The chief looked puzzled again, though he was still smiling a little.

"Massage?" he asked.

"Massages." Carly raised her hands to mime it, then stopped. Could she really mime getting a massage? "Uhhh—" Then she had an idea. She turned and grabbed the guard with the sign, and spun him around so his back was to her. Then she flung him into the wall, raced after him, and began kneading his back. "Massages," she said again.

The chief started cracking up.

"See?" Sam told him. "Massages?" Never one to be left out, she ran over to the big guard and climbed onto a chair right behind him. Then she yanked off his hairpiece! He started to protest, but when she began massaging his bare scalp he stopped complaining. The chief was still laughing as the girls left the guards and faced him again.

"And next thing we knew," Carly explained, "Kyoko and Yuki jumped in their van and ditched us!" She and Sam started spinning around each other and racing around the room, making car noises. They braked to a stop back where they'd started.

"Which made us very sad," Sam told the chief. She and Carly started crying hysterically.

Then the door behind them opened! Two men stepped through, and the first one looked familiar — he had silvery hair and an amused expression.

"Here you are," he announced in what was clearly a British accent.

"Yes, finally!" Carly said with a sigh of relief.

"Hey, it's the iWeb guy from the v-mail!" Sam shouted.

Carly nodded, recognizing him as well. "And he speaks English," she pointed out.

Sam held out her arms to him, thrilled. "Sweet English!" She looked ready to hug him.

Mr. Wilkins laughed. "Indeed," he agreed. Then he said something in Japanese to the security chief, who said something back.

"*iCarly* people," he nodded to include all of them, "come with me!"

Then he led them out of the room. Free at last! And since he was the co-chairman of the iWeb Awards, Carly hoped this meant they'd still get to perform after all!

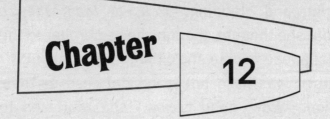

Chapter 12

They followed Mr. Wilkins down a short hallway and then down a longer one. Carly recognized the back stage — she thought it might be the same place where the guards had caught up with them before. But Mr. Wilkins didn't stop there. Instead he led them across that space, right up to the wings — and then he gestured for Carly, Freddie, and Sam to stay with him as he walked out onto the stage!

Carly looked at Sam and Freddie, who looked back at her and shrugged. But Mr. Wilkins was in charge, so if this was what he wanted, that was what they'd do, Carly thought as she followed him onstage —

— and stopped in her tracks.

Man, this place was big! There had to be thousands of people out in the audience! And the minute she and the others appeared, they started cheering and clapping. *Well, at least they're friendly*, she thought, though she remembered the last Japanese people she'd thought that about!

Still, it was hard not to be flattered by their reaction. "Wow, good crowd," she muttered to Sam, who nodded.

The host was motioning for Carly and the others to step forward and join him, and Mr. Wilkins nodded—he was clapping along with everyone else, and turned and headed back offstage as they moved closer to the front.

"Wait," Carly asked the host when the cheers had died down a little bit, "so when do we perform?" That brought a wave of laughter from the audience. "And why was that funny?" she continued.

Through the laughter, the host explained, "You've already won!" He was laughing, too.

Carly and Sam stared at him—Freddie seemed too shocked by the crowd to react. "What do you mean?" the girls asked.

But the host had turned to face the audience instead. "The winners of the iWeb award for Best Web Comedy Show," he announced. "*iCarly!*"

The crowd was going wild, and Carly finally realized this was really happening. "Oh my goodness!" she squealed as their show's title graphics appeared on the big screen behind them. She and Sam hugged, then she hugged Freddie, then he hugged Sam. They were all jumping up and down with excitement. They'd won! She still couldn't quite believe it. "But how did we win?" she insisted.

"They didn't even see us perform," Sam agreed.

But Freddie grinned at them. "Yeah, they did," he told them proudly. Both of the girls asked him how, and his grin got wider. "A little Freddie techno-magic," he explained, tickling Sam till she burst out laughing.

Carly remembered how he'd been fiddling with that panel in the room they'd been stuck in, and how he'd started filming them with his camera — which shot hi-def — and started to figure out what had happened. But she got distracted when a beautiful Japanese woman in a long red gown sashayed across the stage and handed her their iWeb award. It looked exactly like the ones she'd seen in Mr. Wilkins' office on his v-mail, a styl-ized lower-case "i" with the bottom portion solid metal and the dot a faceted crystal ball — and it was theirs!

"Oh my goodness!" she exclaimed again. Spencer and Mrs. Benson were shouting and clapping for them from the wings, right beside Mr. Wilkins.

"Can I touch it?" Sam begged her.

"Yeah," Carly told her at once. "Let's do it!" together they held it up for the crowd and Freddie joined them as everyone rose to their feet and clapped and cheered.

Well, almost everyone — a motion off to the side caught Carly's eye, and she glanced over just in time to see Kyoko and Yuki being led away by police officers. In handcuffs. They were actually lucky that the police found them before Sam did!

She saw someone else familiar, too — a man in a tuxedo and a beret. Henri P'Twa didn't look happy. She saw him glare at his "poopit," Oompé. Then he yelled something at it — Carly couldn't hear what over the crowd, but she suspected it was "stupid poopit!"—hurled it to the ground, and stormed off.

But whatever—she wasn't going to worry about any of that. They'd won! The Japanese woman led them offstage. Mrs. Benson gave all three of them big hugs—even Sam—before returning to the chore of cleaning mud off Freddie's face. Spencer, however, was on his cell phone—another thing Kyoko and Yuki had lied abut, apparently!—and snapped it shut just as Carly ran up to him.

"That's so awesome!" he enthused, giving her a big brotherly squeeze. "But we have to hurry back to the hotel and pack! Our boat leaves in an hour!"

"Oh. Okay." Carly released him and motioned for the others to follow as they headed for the stage door—the same one they'd had so much trouble getting through in the first place. "Wait," she said as his words finally penetrated. "Did you say 'boat'?"

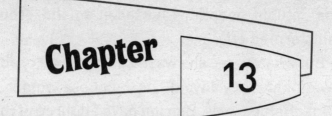

Chapter 13

"**O**hhh, I feel seasick," Mrs. Benson declared, clutching her stomach. For once, Carly couldn't blame her.

"This is horrible," she agreed. So did Sam and Freddie. They were in the hold of a beat-up old fishing trawler, sprawled out or perched on coils of rope, bundled nets, or rickety crates. The entire hold smelled of fish, and the plank floor was slippery from fish oil and fish guts. Not that there was even a guppy in sight at the moment, but it still smelled.

Spencer shook his head. "You guys didn't want to go back on Freight Dog's plane," he reminded them. "And this was the best transportation Socko could get us."

"Well, Socko should stick to selling socks," Carly complained. Somewhere up above, the boat let out one of its long, plaintive horn blasts.

"Don't they have any food on this boat?" Sam wanted to know. Carly was pretty sure she still had a Fat Cake or two stashed in her suitcase, but figured those were probably only for emergencies. Everyone looked around, but they didn't see anything that looked remotely edible — not even for Sam.

"Oh, wait," Spencer said after a second. "I've got a whole bag of Japanese candy!" He reached into his backpack and pulled out a crumpled bag, which he opened and passed around. Mrs. Benson refused to go near any, but the rest of them each took a handful. They were all starving and popped some in their mouth at once —

— and just as quickly spit them out again.

"Uch!" Carly spat, trying to get the waxy film off her tongue. "This is soap!"

Spencer stared at the contents of the bag. "Oh, yeah."

"How long are we stuck on this thing again?" Freddie asked.

"Yeah, how long before it gets us to Seattle?" Carly agreed.

Spencer suddenly busied himself with folding

the bag back up and tucking it away again.

"Spencer?" Carly glared at him. "Spencer, this boat *is* taking us back to Seattle, right?"

"Well," Spencer hedged, "it'll get us home, sure."

"And by 'get us home' you mean — ?" she prompted her brother.

"Socko said they'd let us out near Seattle," Spencer explained quietly.

"What? What does that mean, 'let us out'?" Carly demanded. "Are they taking us back to Seattle or not?"

"I'm not sure they're actually stopping in Seattle, no," Spencer replied.

"So what are we supposed to do then?" Sam demanded. "Swim?"

Carly saw the look on her brother's face. "Oh, you've got to be kidding me!"

"Well, look at the bright side," Spencer told her. "We won't need any parachutes this time!" He didn't say anything else because he was too busy ducking, as Carly, Sam, and Freddie all started pelting him with their half-eaten Japanese soaps.

It was going to be a long, long boat ride.

People of Earth — don't miss a single
iCarly book!

iCarly #1: iHave a Web show!

iCarly #2: iWanna Stay!

iCarly #3: iWant a World Record!

iCarly #4: iAm Famous!

iCarly #5: iAm Your Biggest Fan!